BRIDGERS 6: THE BOND OF ABSOLUTION

STAN C. SMITH

To those who look to the future but don't forget the past.

THE BOND OF ABSOLUTION

If you call me a shitling one more time, I'll knock you out. Maybe I don't have a home, or a family, but someday that's all gonna change.

PASSERINA (INFINITY) FOWLER - 16 YEARS OLD

1
———

BEACH

MAY 2 - 7:58 AM

INFINITY FOWLER ROLLED HER SHOULDERS, trying to loosen muscles that refused to relax. In less than two minutes she would be bridging for the last time. She fidgeted with the language translator on her wrist for a moment and then scanned the ragtag group of fellow migrants surrounding her in the bridging chamber—twenty-two in all, ranging from a Marine and his girlfriend to a former President of the United States and her one-legged husband. It wasn't much of a seed colony for populating an entire world.

A hand grasped hers and squeezed. She turned and gazed into Desmond Weaver's eyes. He forced a smile, but he was obviously edgy. And for good reason. The migrants really had no idea what kind of world they were bridging to. They only had the promises of Kitty, a fuzzy, human-like being who had already proven to be ruthless and judgmental. However, there was no turning back now. For better or worse, Infinity and the others were about to see their new permanent home.

Infinity turned to check on Armando Doyle. The poor guy had his eyes closed, and his lips were moving slightly as if he were saying a prayer. Armando was the oldest person on the team, even older than President Millwright and her husband. He was also the closest thing to a father that Infinity had, so she hoped his body could handle the bridge and whatever might happen after. She then glanced at Lenny Stiles and his wife Isabelle Millwright. Lenny was holding Daisy, their one-year-old daughter. Daisy had bridged to this world a month ago without any problems, but how would she do if things got rough on their new destination world? And then there was Celia Pickett, who was seven months pregnant. Celia was Xavier Cahill's partner, and the two had insisted on being part of the team, in spite of the pregnancy. Fortunately, the team included two doctors, one of which was an obstetrician.

"Are they supposed to come here and help us with this, or what?" Xavier asked.

Infinity released Desmond's hand and shook her head. "Kitty assured me that it would simply happen. At eight o'clock." She turned and looked at the faces around her. "This is the time for my advice speech, but I'm pretty sure my old spiel would be useless now. Bridging these days isn't anything like—"

She fell silent. She squinted and raised a hand to shade her eyes from the sun. A breeze tickled the three-week stubble on her scalp and fluttered through the fabric of her t-shirt and shorts. She still had her clothes, even her shoes. She felt Desmond grasp her hand again.

A delighted giggle erupted from Daisy.

"I'll be damned," said Hayley Millwright, the U.S. President from Infinity's original world. "It's true. Everything Kitty told us is true!"

Infinity's eyes were now adjusting to the brightness, and she turned slowly, taking in the scene. The migrants' boxes of supplies were still stacked neatly to the side, held in place by cargo netting, but the people and boxes were now on a wide stretch of golden sand. Beyond the sand was forest, gradually rising up a low hill, with a taller hill in the distance behind it.

She kept turning. Opposite the forest, waves of greenish water were washing up onto the beach and then withdrawing, creating a strip of wet, sparkling sand. A short distance out from shore, the deeper water turned sky blue, with dark patches of coral reef visible below the surface. An island, lined by another strip of beach with forest beyond, was less than a mile offshore. To the left of that was another island, with another to the right. Beyond those as far as Infinity could see were more forested islands, with no signs of any kind of civilization.

"It really is true," Infinity whispered. She glanced at Armando. He seemed fine. In fact, he was smiling, looking wide-eyed at the scene before him.

Desmond released her hand and pointed. "Look at that, Infinity!"

A shape was breaching the water's surface a few hundred yards offshore—a creature larger than a whale. Its arched back cut through the surface, with numerous evenly-spaced ridges along its length.

"It's beautiful," someone exclaimed.

Infinity stared at the magnificent creature. She squinted. Something about it wasn't right. It was the ridges. They were too symmetrical, too perfect. The creature's back went under the water, and its tail emerged before following the body out of view. Infinity was certain now. It wasn't a creature at all—it was a machine.

The group stood silently for a moment, waiting for the thing to resurface.

Lenny spoke up. "Either I'm high on something, or that wasn't really a whale. Or any other kind of sea creature."

"I noticed it, too," Desmond said. "It was mechanical." He turned to Infinity with his brows raised.

Infinity gritted her teeth and then scanned the area around them. She was still trying to wrap her head around the realization that Kitty's promises appeared to have been sincere. This place looked exactly like what Kitty had described, although Kitty hadn't said anything about mechanical whales. The animal-like machine seemed completely out of place in this otherwise pristine setting. What did it mean? Kitty had informed her that another intelligent species already inhabited this world, and that this species would not be a threat. She had even fitted each migrant with a wrist translator to allow communication. The machine in the water had to have been created by these other beings and therefore shouldn't be a threat either. So why were Infinity's instinctual alarms going off throughout her body, opening wide her adrenaline floodgates?

"We're too exposed here," she said. "We need to get off this beach."

Vic Shepherd said, "I know we're supposed to let these other beings find us, but I agree with Infinity." Vic was one of only two Marines who had survived the brutal trial of extinction forced upon the humans by Kitty's people.

Infinity scanned the water. The machine hadn't surfaced again. She pointed to Emily Sanchez, Steven Irizar, and then Gideon Stead, three former National Guardsmen, all of whom she trusted. "You three get the cargo net off the supply boxes. The rest of us will spread out and find a suitable site to set up a camp where we'll be less exposed." She turned to the others. "Groups of three. Stay close to each other. Even if the beings living here are supposed to be friendly, that doesn't mean there won't be predators, jagged rocks, or a hundred other things that can kill you. We need an area with solid, flat ground that's not visible from the beach or the water."

"Good God, look at that!" exclaimed Alexander Millwright. He was gazing down the beach to the west, away from the rising sun.

Infinity turned. It was a creature—this one real flesh and blood—lumbering out of the surf and up the sand, apparently headed for the forest. Several more of the same species were walking up the beach in the distance beyond this creature, and even more were starting to appear among the waves. Infinity swung around and saw more of the creatures emerging along the beach to the east. Each creature walked on four legs, with its massive belly and thick tail dragging in the sand.

"Uh, heads up, everyone," said Gideon. "One's heading this way. Damn, these things are big."

The creature hauled itself from the surf, apparently with considerable effort, and headed straight up the beach toward the migrants. This one was only fifty yards away, and it now became obvious that its chin was higher than the top of Infinity's head. Even though it was lumbering, it could probably outrun a human if it wanted to.

"Get on top of the supply boxes!" Infinity ordered.

No one had to be told twice. The migrants swarmed up the cargo netting, which started to stretch and pull the boxes over toward them.

"Spread out around the gear!" Desmond cried. But it was too late. The netting came loose from the opposite side, and the migrants collapsed on top of each other, followed by a portion of the boxes. Fortunately, the lighter boxes had been placed on top of the stack.

The creature was now twenty yards away.

Infinity grabbed two people by their arms and hoisted them to their feet. "Move behind the boxes, now!"

The rest of the migrants got up and began scrambling to the back side of the collapsed stack.

Infinity gave one of the stragglers a shove then pressed in

behind the group. She peered around the edge. Now ten yards away, the creature's true size nearly took her breath away. It had to be at least four times the mass of an elephant. Greenish-brown skin, wrinkled and sagging, glistened in the sunlight. Its head was wide and flat, almost like that of a hammerhead shark. Two eyes, perhaps four feet apart, stared straight ahead as it continued waddling forward.

The creature paused only a few yards from the stack of boxes. Infinity considered ordering the migrants to run to the trees and, if possible, climb out of the creature's reach, but something about its single-minded determination to make its way straight up the beach gave her pause. Like the others of its kind to the east and west, it seemed only concerned with getting to the forest.

The monster proceeded forward and began climbing over the boxes.

"Get out of its way!" Infinity cried.

The migrants scattered left and right as the boxes groaned and then gave way under the creature's weight. Survival gear and plastic container fragments shot out in every direction as the creature flattened the entire stack. Apparently oblivious to the humans, the monster plowed right through and continued on its path. Its tail, five feet thick at the base, slid over the devastated boxes, grinding camping gear, jugs of water, and food packets into the sand and leaving behind a trail of mucus-like goo.

The creature proceeded to the forest's edge as if nothing unusual had happened. The migrants stared at their gear and at each other in bewilderment.

"Well, damn!" Gideon said.

Infinity kneeled and pulled a cylindrical bag containing a three-person dome tent out of the sand. Two cracked tent poles protruded through a hole in the bag, and the entire thing was coated in slime.

"Hey, you guys need to come see this!" It was Desmond. He

had followed the creature to the edge of the trees sixty yards away and was staring into the forest.

Infinity dropped the damaged tent and made her way to his side, along with Lenny, Xavier, and a half dozen other migrants.

"Check this out, it's amazing," Desmond said, pointing at the creature's hind legs.

The massive slime monster had pushed its way into the forest and was now resting in a swamp at the base of the hill. The water appeared to be a foot or two deep and was churning with the activity of fish or other aquatic animals that had obviously been disturbed by the intrusion of a monster a million times their size.

"I'm sure it's not finished yet," Desmond said. "Wait for it." His face had a look Infinity had seen many times before—he was fascinated by something, probably something that had no bearing on the group's current dilemma.

Infinity sighed. "Desmond, we don't have time for—"

Her words were cut off by a fart-like explosion from beneath the creature's tail. The water bubbled and splattered as it was displaced by semi-transparent gel. And the gel kept coming, barrelloads of it, squirting out and tumbling over itself as if the monster intended to fill the entire swamp with the stuff. Infinity and the others stepped back as the gel threatened to flow over their feet.

"I've seen a lot of wicked-cool shit in my days," said Lenny, who was now carrying Daisy on his shoulders, "but this may take the proverbial cake."

"It's laying eggs," Xavier said.

Infinity looked closer. The gel was actually riddled with dark, walnut-sized objects, more-or-less evenly spaced throughout the stuff. Presumably these were embryos.

"It's an amphibian," Desmond said. "Something similar to a salamander."

"And a honkin' big one at that," Lenny added.

Infinity shook her head. "Okay, nature lesson is over. We're wasting time if this thing isn't a threat or a food source. It doesn't seem to want to eat us, and it's too big for us to kill."

"Someone forgot to bring her curiosity cap," Lenny said.

Infinity glared at him.

Lenny grimaced. "Sorry, just thought some levity might help."

Another gurgling eruption came from between the monster's hind legs, and the spreading egg mass forced the humans to take a few more steps back.

"Infinity's right," Desmond said. "Let's move what's left of our supplies off the beach and out of sight."

"We need to create a defensible camp," Infinity added. "If all the level ground in the area is swampy like this, we'll have to carry the stuff through the water and up the hill."

They moved away from the egg-laying creature and returned to the others who were already busy gathering the scattered and flattened gear. At this point, some of the giant salamanders up and down the beach were starting to lumber back to the sea, apparently finished laying their eggs, while others were still emerging from the surf and heading for the forest.

"You gotta be kidding me." Vic said. "Grab what you can and move it to the side!"

Infinity turned to look. The monster they'd observed was headed back to the water, dragging itself along the exact same path as before—directly at the supplies.

The migrants began frantically grabbing the remaining boxes and loose items, but there wasn't time. They were forced to stand back helplessly as the creature plowed right over most of the stuff again, crushing lanterns, cookstoves, and water filters, shredding tents and sleeping bags, and grinding everything into the sand.

2

—————

REVELATIONS

MAY 2 - 8:49 AM

DESMOND BALANCED A CRACKED box of gear on his shoulder as he sloshed his way through knee-deep water and amphibian egg jelly. The pinky-sized embryos embedded in the jelly wriggled like dancing apostrophes. It was hard to believe each of these little things could someday grow into a 50,000-pound ocean salamander.

After slogging through a hundred yards of swamp, Desmond staggered up the gradual slope to the dry area Infinity had selected to set up camp. This was the last load. Everyone in the group had carried at least five armloads, including Alexander Millwright, who had been fitted a month ago with a surprisingly-functional prosthetic leg.

Desmond deposited his box beside the jumble of other gear the migrants had hauled up from the beach. Only nine boxes were still intact. The others had suffered damage ranging from minor cracks to complete obliteration. The boxes had each been rated to withstand eight hundred pounds of pressure, but even if they had been twice as strong, it wouldn't have mattered. Several of the migrants were busy sorting the gear into two piles, those items that were still usable and those that were beyond repair. The two piles were about the same size. Unfortunately, every last water jug had been ruptured, and all their drinking water had drained uselessly into the sand.

"What are you two looking for?" Infinity asked. She was standing to Desmond's left, watching two of the *wildcards* sorting through the gear. Wildcards was the title Desmond and Infinity had given to the five migrants who had been added to the group at the eleventh hour. Only a few days before bridging out, Colonel Chislett had insisted that one man and four women—all about thirty years old—join the team. Desmond and Infinity had been allowed to interview the five but only after being told that the newcomers would be joining the team regardless. The name wildcards seemed a good fit because no one was sure what to expect from these five.

One of the wildcards, Latonya Saura, glanced up at Infinity. "Doesn't matter. They're not here anyway." She went back to sifting through the stuff.

Infinity shot Desmond a look, frowning, and then turned back to Latonya. "What's not here?"

Latonya straightened up and exchanged a glance with the other wildcard, Tessa Glover. Tessa sighed loudly and said, "The pistols. We were given six pistols and several thousand rounds of ammunition. The colonel told us to *discreetly* add them to the supply crates. So we did. But now they're all gone. We've looked through everything, and they aren't here."

Desmond could hardly believe what the woman had just said, or how casually she'd said it. He tried to keep his voice low. "Jesus Christ, you two. Do you have any idea—"

"No, they obviously don't have a clue!" Infinity shouted. Some of the other migrants stopped what they were doing and turned to stare. "Kitty specifically instructed us not to bring any weapons," Infinity continued, obviously furious. "Her species is far more advanced than ours—you thought they wouldn't detect the hidden weapons? Are you really that stupid?"

Tessa glared back at her for a moment but then looked down at the ground. "Like I said, we were told to do it. Chislett threatened to remove us from the team if we refused."

Desmond thought the woman's casual use of the colonel's last name without his rank might indicate that the wildcards did not have military backgrounds, a notion that agreed with what they'd claimed in the interview. He said, "It's almost certain that Kitty's sensors detected the weapons. I'm guessing she didn't allow them to bridge with us, something I have no doubt she's capable of doing. They probably fell to the bridging chamber floor the moment we bridged out."

Infinity stepped through the array of equipment and stopped within arm's reach of Tessa. "You really don't have a clue, do you? It didn't even occur to you that trying to defy Kitty's instructions may affect all of us? She may have decided not to keep any of her goddamn promises! This may not even be the world she had promised to bridge us to. We could all die here because of what you've done."

"What's going on?" It was Gibson Blunt, another of the wild-cards and one of several migrants who were now gathering around.

"Did you know about the guns?" Infinity asked Gibson.

He shook his head, frowning. "What guns?"

"The others don't know," said Latonya. "Chislett talked to me and Tessa—no one else."

Both of the guilty women were glaring at Infinity with an inten-sity that made Desmond nervous. All five of the wildcards were obviously physically fit, which was one of the reasons he had suspected they might be military, and now they didn't seem intimi-dated much by Infinity's aggression.

Gibson turned to the two women. "And you didn't tell me about this?"

The women's glares faltered for a moment. "We didn't want to jeopardize the whole thing," Tessa said. "We wanted you to have plausible deniability, which you now have."

"For the love of RHF!" Gibson said, almost growling. "You didn't want to jeopardize the whole thing?"

Infinity got up in Tessa's face. "I'm going to hold both of you responsible for whatever consequences you've caused."

Tessa put a hand on Infinity's chest and pushed her away. "You're not in charge."

Desmond knew Infinity was on the verge of violence, but his eyes were drawn to Gibson, who was shaking his head at Latonya, obviously signaling her to stay out of it.

Infinity whipped her right foot behind Tessa's legs and took the woman down with a sweep of her right arm. Tessa hit the ground, but she skillfully rolled into Infinity's legs and pulled her off her feet. Infinity went down hard but then thrust out an elbow, jabbing Tessa in the face hard enough to snap the woman's head back. Within two seconds, Infinity was on top of Tessa and had landed another fierce blow to her face. She gripped the woman's shirt and drew her fist back. "Where did you learn to fight like that? Who the hell are you?"

Tessa, blood flowing from her nose, sneered up at Infinity. "Has anyone told you that you have trust issues?"

Infinity hit her again, eliciting several gasps from the watching migrants.

"She's had enough!" Gibson said. "We're all on the same team here, Infinity."

Desmond stepped forward and put a hand on Infinity's shoulder. "She can't explain herself if she's unconscious."

Infinity shook him off. "Talk," she growled at Tessa.

Tessa squeezed her eyes shut for a moment, obviously dazed by the blows. "We believe in staying in shape and we train for hand-to-hand fighting. Just like you."

"Who's *we*?"

"Us! The five of us you call wildcards. Yeah, I've overheard you using that word."

Infinity pulled on her shirt. "Are you military?"

"No. *God* no!" Tessa glanced over at Gibson.

Gibson said, "Before joining your team, we belonged to a collective—a *guild*, so to speak. Nothing nefarious, just a community of like-minded people with the desire to live by our own philosophies. Self-defense training is important to us, something we thought you'd consider to be valuable."

"So you belong to a cult," Infinity said.

Gibson shook his head. "No, and I take offense at the use of that word."

"I don't give a damn what you take offense to. Your group has jeopardized this entire colony."

"To be honest, I have no knowledge of any guns. If Tessa and Latonya have really done this, then you need to let me discipline them. It's my place to do so."

Infinity's eyes met Desmond's. "They belong to a damn cult," she muttered.

Tessa spoke up. "Like we said, Chislett gave us the guns and told us to hide them in the boxes. But now it doesn't matter. The guns aren't even here."

Infinity finally released Tessa's shirt and stood over her.

Desmond decided she had cooled down enough that he might be able to steer the incident in a different direction. "There are only twenty-two of us in this colony. Every life is valuable beyond measure. One way or another, we all have to end up on the same page. Without harming each other." He gazed directly at Tessa and then at Gibson. "Do the five of you have any intention of harming us or sabotaging our efforts to establish a peaceful life here?"

"Of course not," Gibson replied.

"Then this incident should be set aside for now. We'll sort it all out later. Here's the way I see it. The attempt to defy Kitty's request shouldn't have happened. But it did. And now we have to deal with the consequences. Since we weren't immediately killed for the attempt, I see two possibilities. First, Kitty bridged us to the originally-intended destination. If so, we need to establish a safe, defensible camp and be prepared for eventually encountering the other sentient species that Kitty told us would be here. Second, Kitty bridged us to a different world, perhaps intending for us to die here. If so, we still need to establish a safe, defensible camp and be prepared for whatever comes next. Do all of you understand what I'm saying?"

"You're saying we need to work together," Gibson replied. "I agree."

Desmond eyed Tessa. "Do you understand?"

She nodded.

"Desmond's right," Infinity said.

Desmond then turned to the gathered migrants, making eye contact with each of them until he got a nod or a verbal confirmation. He put his hand back on Infinity's shoulder. "Maybe we should help her up."

Infinity extended a hand. Tessa took it and got to her feet. She stepped back, wiping the blood from her face and refusing to break eye contact with Infinity. "I want to survive here as much as you do. We shouldn't have hidden the guns."

Infinity gave her a curt nod and turned her back on her. "Let's get this camp set up," she said, loud enough for everyone to hear.

"What did we miss?"

Desmond turned to see Gideon, Emily, and Steven approaching. The three former National Guardsmen had been out scouting the surrounding area.

"It's a long story," Infinity replied. "I'll fill you in later."

Gideon hesitated, eyeing Tessa's blood-stained face. "Well, there's something you need to see."

Desmond knew Gideon well enough to sense alarm in the man's tone. Infinity and some of the others must have sensed it too, because they all fell silent. Without another word, the three guardsmen turned and led the entire group to the east.

After making their way through a few hundred yards of forest, Desmond spotted something moving in the trees to the right and slightly up the hillside. "What is that?" he called ahead to the guardsmen.

The group stopped. Emily Sanchez said, "Yeah. Those things have been following us. We had four of them within ten yards at one point. No idea what they are, but they seem harmless enough."

Desmond heard a rustling sound behind him and spun around. A creature the size of a young chimpanzee—maybe forty pounds— was moving through the branches, advancing rapidly toward the humans. It stopped at about fifteen yards, clinging to the side of a thick trunk, and stared.

"Well, crap on a cracker," Lenny said. "Like nothing I've ever seen. Is that a frog?"

The creature's glistening skin was mottled with green and gray. Two forearms, at least twice the length of the hind legs, gripped the tree's bark with clawed fingers. The thing's mouth extended from one side of its face to the other, like a frog's. Its forward-facing eyes were small and black. But unlike a frog, the creature had a discern-able neck, and it quickly turned its head from side to side as it looked at one human and then another. The thing definitely wasn't a frog, but it was certainly amphibian-like. Perhaps it was an amphibian that had evolved to occupy the same niche that monkeys had occupied on Desmond's own world.

The monkey-frog opened its mouth and let out a sound not too different from a crow's caw. Seconds later, the call was answered by dozens of other creatures hidden in the surrounding trees.

"What makes you think they aren't dangerous?" Infinity asked.

"Nothing specific," Gideon replied, "other than the fact that they've left us alone so far. Let's move. What we have to show you isn't far."

Desmond's eyes lingered on the creature as the group resumed walking. He knew what Infinity was thinking. In spite of the conflict over the guns, she was thinking the group needed to start producing primitive weapons for defense. Unfortunately, Desmond agreed.

After another hundred yards, the guardsmen stopped and pointed at the ground. The migrants gathered around.

Before them was the tattered remains of a tent, or some similar kind of shelter. The tent fabric was mostly green, and scattered about were two-foot-long black rods connected in the shape of triangles. Some of these triangles were still connected to each other and attached to the fabric, obviously once a framework for support. On the ground beside this tent was another tent, also flattened and torn. Desmond scanned the area and spotted at least five more.

"Someone set up a camp here," Gideon said. "Looks to be a few months ago, maybe a year." He pulled aside some of the fabric, exposing more shredded fabric that may have once been a sleeping bag or pad. There were also several devices, including two black, concave plates or bowls. Gideon picked up a black disk with a white dome over one side. The other side of the disk had a strap. Gideon slid his hand into the strap, and it appeared to fit perfectly. He touched something on the disk and the white dome began to glow. The glow increased, and seconds later it was too bright to stare at. "A flashlight," Gideon said. "Never seen one like this, though."

Emily held out a dirt-crusted device about five inches long. "We found this in one of the tents."

Desmond immediately recognized it. He took it from her and

held it beside the much-cleaner translator on his own wrist. The two devices were of the same design.

"There's more," Emily said. "Come check this out."

The three guardsmen walked toward the far end of the abandoned camp. As Desmond followed, he stepped over pieces of strange-looking equipment, lengths of rope, and several more tents.

"Holy crap," someone exclaimed.

Desmond caught up to the others. Gideon was holding up the fabric of yet another tent, and beneath it was a jumble of white bones. The bones had been picked clean by microbes, insects, or some other scavengers, and some of them had even been gnawed to the point of being unrecognizable. Three human skulls lay among the bones.

Without hesitating, Lenny kneeled and picked up one of the skulls and stared into its empty eye sockets.

"Dude, parasites," said Xavier. "These people may have been wiped out by a disease, and you're handling their remains?"

Desmond stared at the skull and then looked at one of the others still on the ground. "They weren't human," he said.

The others fell silent, staring.

"Des is right," said Lenny. He picked up the skull's lower jaw—the mandible—and fitted it under the skull's maxilla. He turned the skull for all to see. It was human-like, but it definitely wasn't human. The lower jaw spread outward below the mouth, becoming even broader than the skull's cheekbones. The eye sockets were noticeably smaller than human eyes. Most bizarre, though, were the teeth. Each tooth had been filed to a point, or perhaps these teeth were naturally pointed. Embedded in the front surface of each tooth was a small, glittering stone or jewel of some kind. Even the molars, which would not normally be visible, were festooned with jewels.

Lenny frowned and turned the skull to a specific angle, focusing on something. "And these fat-chinned mofos didn't die from disease. Check this out." He dropped the mandible and placed a finger near the skull's temple.

"Let me see that," Desmond said. Lenny handed him the skull and Desmond held it up. Three perfectly round holes, each only a few millimeters across, penetrated the bone just behind the eye socket. He flipped the skull around. Three more identical holes, entrance or exit wounds, went through the bone above the ear. He glanced at one of the other skulls and immediately saw a similar hole through the forehead.

Desmond turned to Infinity. "They were shot."

3

———————

CACOPHONY

MAY 2 - 9:54 AM

INFINITY INSPECTED THE TERRAIN. She was standing on a relatively flat area of the hillside. On the downhill side was a rocky bluff, a vertical drop of about fifteen feet, which extended at least a hundred yards to the east and to the west. If something or someone approached from downhill, the migrants would have an elevated defensive position.

Sixty yards from the bluff, on the uphill side, was a jumble of bus-sized boulders. Only two paths through the boulders had proven to be easily passable, which meant only two pinch points would need to be defended from an attack from uphill. It also meant the migrants had two routes for retreat up the hill.

"This is the spot," she announced. "It's the best we've found."

Desmond and Gideon glanced at each other as if they were each encouraging the other to speak up.

Infinity crossed her arms. "What? You don't like it?"

Desmond scratched the stubble on his scalp. "Yeah, I like it.

But we're probably a half mile from our gear. The others are already tired and on edge. Do you really think it's worth making the move?"

"Yes."

Another annoying glance between the two men. Finally, they both shrugged.

"Then let's go share the good news," Desmond said, forcing a smile.

Gideon massaged his shoulder, which had been severely injured on the lemur world but had been miraculously patched up by Kitty and was now nearly healed.

Infinity let her arms drop. "You two go on back and get the others organized. I'm going to start clearing some of this ground for tents."

Yet another annoying glance between the two men.

"I'll go back," Gideon said. "You two get started here." Before anyone could respond, he turned and started jogging toward the east end of the bluff below them.

They watched him disappear among the trees.

She shot Desmond a look. "Okay, what?"

"You seem a little on edge, Passerina," he said, using her birth name since they were now alone. He stepped forward and held out his arms.

Infinity hesitated for a moment but then thought, what the hell, why not? She closed the distance between them and they embraced. She relaxed and let her head rest on his shoulder while he did the same on hers. Several minutes passed in silence, and Infinity felt her tension gradually recede. She realized he was pushing subtle visions into her mind, an ability he'd acquired two years ago on a different world. Instead of protesting this mental intrusion, she just let it happen. Visions of almost-placid waves rolling up and back on a beach similar to the one a short distance from where they now stood. People—perhaps their fellow migrants

—in flowing white garments, walking hand in hand along the beach. Laughing children playing barefoot at the water's edge.

She inhaled, closed her eyes, and allowed herself several more minutes of this bliss.

Desmond was the one to finally pull away. He gazed at her. "We're going to make this work. At least here we don't have four-hundred-pound tiger beetles chasing us down."

She tried to smile but then wasn't sure her mouth had even moved. "Damn right we'll make it work."

He pulled away even more, and she was tempted to yank him back into her arms—to hold him for just another few seconds. Instead, she sighed and let go. "I think we can use what's left of the gear boxes to create a bunker." She pointed. "Using that gap between the boulders."

He turned to look. "Might work. We've got a fair amount of tape and paracord for construction." He turned back and studied her face. "I'm going on the assumption that Kitty hasn't reneged on her promise. This is the place we're supposed to be."

"I imagine that's exactly what those other beings told themselves, the ones now rotting in their wrecked camp."

"I can't explain that yet, and neither can you," he said. "Perhaps we'll eventually learn what happened."

"Kitty's people have *consequences* for breaking their rules, remember? They destroy entire worlds. They wipe out civilizations. Hell, right now they may be destroying the world we just bridged from, killing everyone and everything on it. Just because those idiots tried to bring six handguns."

Desmond blinked. "Well... thanks for inserting that hellish concept into my brain."

Infinity huffed out a brief laugh. "I guess we'll never know." She was tired of talking and began clearing the ground of loose rocks and fallen limbs.

After several minutes working at this task in silence, they had cleared enough ground for the tents, especially considering several of the tents were now only good for cannibalizing spare parts.

Infinity tossed aside a few more sticks then glanced up and saw six migrants approaching from the east along the top edge of the bluff carrying loads of gear. Gideon was in the lead, and Infinity gritted her teeth when she realized all five of the wildcards were following him.

Desmond stepped up to Infinity's side. "Well, this should be interesting."

"Gideon should have known better than to venture away from the group by himself with those five," she said.

As they approached, Infinity pointed to the ground beside one of the boulders, and the migrants deposited their loads there.

Gideon eyed Infinity. "Gibson says he wants to talk to you two."

"I feel we owe you an apology," Gibson said, stepping forward. "We were not entirely honest with you at the beginning of this endeavor. We meant no harm by it. We want to assure you that we intend to do whatever we can to make this colony a success."

Infinity eyed the four women one at a time. They all had that same look of self-assurance that had made Infinity suspicious in the first place. Tessa's nose was now red and swollen, but the bleeding had stopped.

"Why didn't you simply tell the truth?" Desmond asked.

"We've been told that you are not from our world," Gibson replied. "Our timeline diverged from your own over twenty years ago. I'm sure you're aware that red howler fever drastically changed the nature of the United States in our timeline, but you may not be aware of the extent of division and tribalism that resulted. Our survival depended upon isolating ourselves from the infected. By necessity, people joined together with those they trusted. Some of these groups sought out remote rural locations, while others barricaded themselves within houses or buildings in the cities and suburbs. Some of these groups were poorly matched, resulting in internal betrayal and even violence. Others were well matched and became close-knit families." He gestured toward Desmond, then Infinity, and then Gideon. "From what I've heard, you people formed your own tight-knit family while you were stranded in another timeline for the last two years. Am I right?"

"You heard about it because we didn't lie about it," Infinity said.

Gibson grimaced slightly. "Fair enough." He nodded toward the four women beside him. "My companions and I were lucky. Our community was solid. In fact, we, along with nearly a hundred others, decided to remain as a community even after the threat of RHF had diminished. Even after the government passed a federal law banning guilds such as ours." He shook his head and rolled his eyes. "A misguided attempt to bring everyone back together, to heal the country. But we didn't want to split up. You see, like many of the other guilds, we had developed our own rules and traditions. Ones that didn't necessarily mesh with society's new standards."

Infinity said, "Such as?"

Gibson hesitated. "Preparing ourselves for violence, for example. We didn't know how far things would go with RHF. It could have set us back to the Stone Age, and we were ready for that."

"What about polygamy?" Desmond asked.

Infinity shot a glance at Desmond. She hadn't even thought of that.

Again Gibson hesitated, while the four women stared at Desmond with faces of stone.

"Tessa, Latonya, Sue, and Donica are my mates," Gibson said matter-of-factly. "However, we are not married. Humans, in a more natural state such as what could have resulted from the RHF pandemic, tend to be a male-dominant species. As with many other large mammal species, male humans have an innate tendency to fight for mates, with the strongest winning the spoils." Again he gestured to the women.

Infinity reviewed his words in her mind to make sure she hadn't misheard. "You've got to be kidding. You fought other men for these women?"

"Fought and killed, if you must know."

Infinity felt her hands becoming fists, and she tried to control her breathing. "If you think for one goddamn minute that you're going to push your crazy-ass ideas onto this colony, then you and your harem are on your own, starting right now."

Gibson held up his hands, palms out. "Infinity, that's not our—"

"Wait!" Gideon said. "Do you hear that?"

A distant sound abruptly rose above the furious gushing of blood in Infinity's ears. It was the crowing call of those bizarre creatures Desmond called monkey-frogs—a *lot* of monkey-frogs. Maybe hundreds of them. The sounds were coming from the direction of the other migrants. Several human shouts rose among the cacophony.

"Something's wrong," Infinity said. Without another word she sprinted toward the east end of the bluff. Desmond and the others quickly followed.

The cawing increased in volume as they got closer, and several minutes later they came upon the initial camp site. The site appeared to be completely surrounded by countless screaming monkey-frogs. The humans were clustered together in the center of the clearing trying to scare the creatures off by waving their arms and shouting. So far the monkey-frogs were keeping their distance. The collective sound and behavior of the amphibians made Infinity think of the times when she had been in the forest near SafeTrek and would see hundreds of crows antagonizing an owl. The crows usually didn't physically attack the owl, but if they had, they certainly could have overwhelmed it by sheer numbers.

Infinity picked up a dead, six-foot tree limb as she approached the perimeter of enraged monkey-frogs. She turned to Desmond, Gideon, and the wildcards and gestured for them to do the same. When they were all armed with sticks, she pointed toward the camp, nodded her head once, and charged forward, wielding her weapon. As they closed in on the creatures from behind, Infinity swung at the lowest one she could find, but it was still too high for her to make contact.

Desmond slammed his stick against the tree's trunk and shouted, "Get out of here!"

Gideon and the wildcards followed his lead and began shouting and hitting the trees.

This seemed to infuriate the creatures even more, and more monkey-frogs around the camp perimeter began swarming toward this new disturbance.

"Grab any sticks you can find and take them to the others!" Infinity commanded. Then, as difficult as it was to ignore the vocal attacks from above, she gathered up four more sticks and ran to the center of the camp. "Take these and be ready to use them!"

Seconds later, all twenty-two migrants except one-year-old Daisy were armed with crude weapons and standing in a defensive circle facing outward.

Several long minutes passed as they waited, watching the monkey-frogs cawing and shaking the tree limbs. But gradually the cacophony died out and the creatures began wandering off, jumping from tree to tree. About half of them headed to the west as a group, and the other half headed to the east.

Finally, some of the migrants began dropping their sticks.

A timid voice said, "Every person from my version of Earth has learned more about howler monkeys than we care to know. You know, because of red howler fever." It was Reyna, Vic's girlfriend. Infinity hadn't heard the girl speak since she and Desmond had interviewed her several weeks before. Reyna went on. "Howler monkeys defend their territory by howling loudly at intruders."

"Louder than freaking hell," Vic added.

"Maybe these things are like howler monkeys," Reyna said. "You know, because they made a ruckus but didn't actually attack us. It's possible they weren't even yelling at *us*, at least not to begin with. It looked to me like there were two groups. Maybe we just happened to be in the middle of a territory dispute."

"I like this chick!" Lenny said. "She's a glass-half-full kind of gal, like Isabelle and me. Vic, you're a lucky man."

Infinity was still gripping her stick weapon, and she held it up. "As nice as it might be to believe they aren't dangerous, we have to assume that next time they might attack. We also have to assume there are dangerous creatures here that we haven't encountered yet. Not to mention whatever beings created that machine we saw in the water. We don't even know for sure yet if Kitty bridged us to the world she promised us." She shot Gibson a look. "We need weapons—spears for now, and eventually maybe bows. We brought axes and survival knives, but those can only be used for close-quarters combat." She pointed at Tessa and then at Latonya. "Since you were so determined to bring weapons here, I want you two to be in charge of producing twenty-two spears five to six feet long. If you can make use of some of the broken equipment, that's fine. Are you good with that assignment?"

Both women turned to Gibson.

"Don't look at him!" Infinity said. "He doesn't own you, in spite of what he might think. I'm asking *you*."

Tessa narrowed her eyes at Infinity, but then she nodded. "I'll help out any way you want."

"So will I," Latonya said.

Gibson raised a hand. "And I'd like to help them. We're accustomed to working as a team, and more hands will get the job done faster."

Infinity considered this. Then she scanned the other migrants until her eyes met Steven Irizar's. She trusted the former guardsman, just as she trusted all the members of her colony from the arthropod world. Steven apparently understood what she had in mind and nodded. "I'll help them with the task, Infinity."

Sue said, "Donica and I would like to help with that too."

Infinity replied, "Are you capable of doing anything at all without Gibson there to guide you?"

"Of course we are," Sue replied. "You're making assumptions about us without—"

"Then you can help move the gear," Infinity interrupted. "Steven, Gibson, Tessa, and Latonya will fashion the spears."

Both Sue and Donica glanced at Gibson, who gave them a nod. Infinity exhaled in frustration. Even when directly confronted about their ability to act independently, the two women sought the asshole's approval.

Infinity then spoke to the others. "Gideon's probably told you that we found a much more defensible site a short ways up the slope. I now believe even more than before that we need to move up there. I assume you're all okay with that. Am I right?"

A chorus of acknowledgements confirmed they agreed.

"Hey, you guys," said Xavier, "Celia, Lenny, and I have been working with the water filters, trying to fill some of the bladders. It's warm here, and with all our drinking water gone we'll be getting dehydrated soon. Problem is, the water in the swamp has so much crap suspended in it that the filters get clogged within seconds. We tried back-flushing the filters but can't even get enough clean water to do that effectively. We walked to the east as far as we dared, and then to the west, but we couldn't find a clear-flowing stream. There's just nothing but swamps between the beach and the hills in both directions. I, for one, have no intention of drinking that water unfiltered."

Vic said, "What about them hand-operated desalinators? We brought six. Two were destroyed by that fat-ass whale-salamander, but the other four looked okay to me. They'll remove the salt from the ocean water. They ain't easy to use—take a lot of pumping—but they might do until we find a better source of fresh water." He stepped over to one of the equipment boxes. "I'll get 'em out."

Xavier eyed Infinity. "It's probably our best option for now."

She let out a frustrated grunt. They'd have to go back to the beach to do this.

Desmond nudged her elbow. "You and I can help with the water while Gideon coordinates the move to the new site."

"That's a plan," Gideon said forcefully. He turned and faced the pile of gear. "Let's get started. This shit isn't going to move itself."

4

DESALINATION

MAY 2 - 11:31 AM

DESMOND FELT REVITALIZED by the brightness of the unshaded beach. He also felt exposed and vulnerable, no doubt due to Infinity's interminable attitude that the worst-case scenario was about to occur. He could see no giant salamanders now—apparently their synchronized egg-laying session was over—and the beach looked peaceful and inviting.

Desmond, Infinity, Lenny, Xavier, and Vic stopped just out of reach of the advancing and retreating waves.

Vic removed a few rubber bands from one of the four hand-operated desalination filters. He then reached for one of the ten or so transparent four-liter bladders Xavier was carrying and pushed the end of a flexible tube from the pump into the bladder's nozzle until it snapped into place. "Clean water hose," he said. "Ain't nothing much to this other than endless pumping," He pointed to a second tube extending from the pump. "Dirty water hose. Put the end of it in the water and then pump the handle like this." He held the tubular body of the device in his left hand and started pumping an attached lever with his right. "These ain't your basic freshwater pumps, though. It'll take a half hour of work to fill this bladder with salt-free water."

Infinity let out an annoyed growl. "A half hour?" She turned her head, scanning the sea and beach. "Alright, we'll use all four pumps at once, fill up four bags, and get back to the camp. That's sixteen liters of water. That's, um...."

"About seven-tenths of a liter per person," Desmond offered. "It's not enough. If we pump for an hour we can double that."

Infinity scanned the area again. "An hour is a long time to be out here. Seven-tenths of a liter each should get us by until we find a better freshwater source."

Desmond could see that she was determined. "Alright, we'll get started and then see how it goes. Okay?"

Infinity nodded. She held out her hand. "Give me one of those pumps."

Vic handed her the one he'd already prepared. "Uh, there's one other thing. The shallow water here in this surf is churning too much sediment. You won't be able to filter it. We'll have to get out into deeper water. The deeper, the better."

"You're kidding," Infinity said.

Desmond gazed out at the sea. At about a hundred yards out, the greenish water transitioned to clear blue. How deep would it be out there?

Xavier said, "Since I'm actually sane, I have a problem with this."

Lenny picked up one of the desalination pumps and began assembling it. "Where's your sense of adventure, Xavier? It'll be a goddamn zip-banging thrill. A chance to see marine creatures no human has ever seen. That's why I brought these." He tucked the pump under one arm and pulled from his pocket several pairs of swim goggles. He handed them out. "I pictured us taking a gander at the sea life in knee-deep water but, hell, if we have to go out to our necks, all the better, right?"

Desmond held his goggles up by the head strap. The thought of seeing totally new species of fish and other aquatic life was certainly enticing. But watching an open mouth filled with teeth rushing toward him—not so much.

Infinity stretched her goggles over her head but then pushed them past her face until they hung from her neck. "Okay, I'm going alone first. I'll go out up to my waist and start pumping. You guys watch the water. If you don't see anything after several minutes, then three of you bring the other filters out." She pulled her translator off her wrist and handed it to Xavier. "Xavier, you stay on the beach and watch for anything moving our way in the water. You'll have a better view than we will." She turned and started wading through the surf.

A rush of panic rippled through Desmond's body. "Wait, why should you go out there first?"

"Too late," she said over her shoulder. "I already called it. Shout if you see anything."

Desmond groaned and then fumbled with his pump, ripping off the rubber bands and attaching the clean-water hose and then the dirty-water hose while glancing up frequently at the water.

Infinity had walked out at least forty yards before the water covered her waist. Without glancing back, she began pumping her desalinator, her right shoulder and elbow heaving with each stroke.

"I really don't think I could do that," Xavier said.

Lenny snorted. "You gotta ask yourself, are you a man or a mouse?" He put a hand to his ear. "What was that? Did I just hear you squeak?"

Desmond didn't take his eyes off the water. "Are you guys even watching?"

Infinity turned to them and held up the empty bladder at the end of her clean-water tube. "I don't think it's working."

"It's too silty there," Vic said. "You're going to have to go on out."

This was too much for Desmond. "She can't be a hundred yards out there on her own." He pulled his goggles over his head and around his neck, handed his translator to Xavier, and headed out to join her.

Seconds later, Lenny and Vic were sloshing through the surf behind him.

"You guys need to remember," Lenny said, "even off the beaches of Florida, which was the shark-attack capital of the world, the chances of being attacked were almost nil. Nada. Zip. Zero. Zilch. It's all in the statistics."

"How about we just don't even talk about it?" Vic said.

By the time they had caught up with Infinity, Desmond was in shoulder-deep water. Infinity was in up to her chin, holding her device awkwardly above the surface while trying to pump it.

"It should still work if you hold it under the water," Vic said. "You'll wear your arms out doing that."

She lowered the filter. "At least it's starting to fill the bag now. I guess you guys didn't like my idea of watching from the beach until you knew it's safe."

Desmond checked the connections of his tubes and then started pumping. "Just trying to speed up the process."

Lenny positioned his goggles over his eyes and put his head under. About thirty seconds later he threw his head back and sucked in air. "Check out the schools of fish on the bottom! I'm the first human to see them, so I get to come up with their name."

Desmond couldn't pass this up. He tucked his pump under one arm, worked his goggles up over his eyes, and bent his knees, which submerged his head. Through surprisingly clear water, he saw hundreds of six-inch, sand-colored fish darting around in unison just above the substrate. Each time one of the humans moved a foot, the creatures would scatter, only to return a few seconds later.

He squinted at the nearest fish. It actually had four tiny legs, allowing it to maneuver around slowly on the sand. He shoved his foot toward it, causing the creature to flick its tail and dart away, tucking its legs against its body and then spreading them again as it came to a stop. Desmond straightened to his full height and exhaled.

"Did you see they have legs? I'm not sure they're fish."

"Maybe amphibians of some kind," Lenny said before going back under.

"Is this what you consider speeding up the process?" Infinity asked.

Desmond flashed a grimace. "Just one more look." He bent his knees again. Below the surface, he looked to the east and then to the west. The flat, sandy bottom extended uniformly in both directions as far as the water's visibility would allow him to see. Several schools of torpedo-shaped fish or fish-like creatures hung in the water column, keeping their distance from the humans. They were only about two feet long, probably too small to be a threat.

Desmond turned and gazed away from the beach toward deeper water. He could barely see the outlines of coral formations, perhaps sixty yards farther out. It would be a fascinating area to explore once the colony became safely established, and he hoped that the half-dozen sets of snorkels, masks, and fins Lenny had insisted on packing hadn't been destroyed by the lumbering whale-salamander.

As he started to rise to the surface, he saw movement. A dark shape was swimming steadily from right to left between the humans and the coral formations. He couldn't see any details, but the creature appeared to be about the size and shape of a dolphin. There was another one, following behind the first. Desmond looked to the left and right of the creatures, trying to see if there were more, but he needed air.

He surfaced and took a few breaths. "I don't want to be an

alarmist, but there are some pretty big fish moving around out there." He pointed toward the corals.

Lenny ducked under to take a look.

"How big?" Infinity asked.

He shook his head. "At least three hundred pounds. Maybe bigger."

Lenny's head popped up. "I saw at least four, swimming back and forth about forty yards out. I don't like it, regardless of what I said about statistics."

Infinity turned and gazed out over the deeper water but didn't put her goggles on. "Alright, this isn't worth it. We'll have to get water a different way." She turned toward shore.

"Hey!" Xavier cried out from the beach. He was waving his hands, and then he pointed to Desmond's left. "Get back here, now!"

Desmond's chest tightened. He pulled his goggles down and turned to his left to look. He expected to see something like shark fins approaching, but there was nothing visible. He kept turning, and then he saw it. Out in the deeper water, a machine had surfaced—a mechanical whale like the one he and the other migrants had seen just after bridging here. The thing was massive, at least double the size of the whale-salamanders.

"Looks like our friend is back," Vic said, staring at the object. "Since that thing ain't moving, I'm guessing this time it spotted us."

Infinity mumbled an incomprehensible curse. "One problem at a time. First we need to get out of the water." She started making her way back to the beach.

Desmond placed his goggles back over his eyes and went under. Almost immediately the tightening in his chest exploded into full-blown alarm. The dolphin-sized creatures had multiplied, and now they were closer. At least six were zig-zagging no more than thirty yards away. One of them abruptly stopped swimming and sank to the bottom. As Desmond watched, four legs unfolded from the creature's side. It began slowly walking closer. A movement to the right caught Desmond's eye and he turned. More of the legged dolphins were approaching. He kept turning. They were now on all sides, even blocking the group's retreat to the beach.

He popped his head up. "Stop! We've got a real problem. Now we're surrounded."

Infinity positioned her goggles over her eyes and went under to look. Several seconds later she was back up. "Shit! Move closer together. Line up shoulder to shoulder. It'll make them think we're a larger animal as we walk to the beach."

Desmond kept his goggles in place as he sidled up to the others. Still awkwardly holding his filter, he put his arms around Infinity's and Lenny's shoulders. He pushed his face down into the water. Now, no more than fifteen yards away, three of the creatures were walking on the bottom, steadily creeping closer. Their movements appeared slow and deliberate, but he was sure that a few powerful swipes of their tails would propel them that distance within a second or two. Feeling out of his element and completely helpless, Desmond's panic nearly overwhelmed him. He lifted his head. "They're not backing off!"

Infinity clenched his shoulder painfully. "They might when we get closer. Keep moving."

"They're coming at us from behind!" Vic cried.

Desmond glanced back. Two creatures were shooting toward them, their broad backs breaching the surface. He released Infinity and spun around.

"Fight them off!" Infinity shouted.

Desmond slapped the water with his arms and yelled, "Back off!" One of the predators was coming straight for him, and he raised his fist, hoping to land a blow on its snout. When the crea-ture was only a few feet away, it began violently spinning, like a crocodile doing a death roll. But this creature didn't have its intended prey in its mouth. The beast beside it stopped its forward progress and turned. Desmond could actually see one of its fist-sized eyes watching its writhing companion.

The first creature continued spinning, churning the water's surface. The foaming water was now pink, bloody from a wound somewhere on the animal's body.

The second creature lunged in and clamped its teeth into its wounded companion, stopping the rotation.

Desmond realized his team was much too close to this conflict. He grabbed Infinity's arm. "Move back!"

More dark shapes rushed past the humans, one of them actually brushing against Desmond's leg, as the other predators joined in the attack, apparently attracted by the blood. Within seconds, the injured creature was being torn to bits.

"The beach," Infinity ordered. "Move it!"

Instead of walking, Vic and Lenny started swimming frantically for shore.

Desmond glanced at Infinity and their eyes met.

"I'll bring up the rear," she said.

He shook his head.

She narrowed her eyes and let out a curse but took off swimming.

Desmond let her get a few yards ahead and swam after her, fully aware that he would be the one to become the center of another feeding frenzy if any of the creatures decided to pursue them.

He swam without daring to look back. Stroke after stroke, the shore slowly drew closer. He glimpsed Vic and Lenny getting to their feet and running up the beach. Then Infinity was on her feet. Desmond's fingertips brushed against the sandy bottom. He took two more strokes and then pulled his knees under him and ran, grunting and pushing his legs through the surf. Then his feet sloshed through ankle-deep water. Finally, he was on dry sand. He stood beside Infinity, hands on his knees, sucking in oxygen.

"You need to turn around and look at what I'm seeing," said Xavier.

Desmond straightened up and turned. Bloody water still churned at the site of the feeding creatures. Beyond that was the whale-machine, but now it looked different.

Desmond wiped the water and sand from his eyes. Creatures of some kind were standing on top of the machine. Definitely not humans—their proportions were wrong. In fact, their proportions were *very* wrong. Each of them stood on two absurdly long legs, which were bent at the knee, and the two knees protruded upward higher than each creature's head. As Desmond stared, he decided the two legs might actually be arms. It looked like the creatures also had tails, possibly even two tails. One thing he was sure of was that they were staring toward the shore, either watching the feeding frenzy or watching the humans. Or both.

Xavier said, "I guess now we know what the whale-machine is—a submarine."

"They've seen us," Lenny said, "No point in running away now."

"Until they attack us," Infinity added.

Desmond couldn't take his eyes off the creatures on the sub's deck, almost wishing they would come closer for a better look. He had seen bizarre animals on the various versions of Earth he'd visited, but these things had a body shape unlike any of them. "These guys have to be the other sentient beings we were supposed to meet."

"Only if Kitty sent us to the version of Earth she originally promised," Infinity countered.

Desmond finally pulled his eyes away from the beings when he noticed a dark shape emerging from the surf onto the beach—one of the creatures that had almost killed them. The thing was now walking on all fours. Out of the water, it became more obvious the creature was salamander-like, with scaleless, rippled skin. But its toothy mouth was as menacing as that of any crocodile. Behind the creature several more elongated backs were just breaking the surface, all moving toward the humans. He and the others started backing up.

"This freakin' place is just one trippy confrontation after another," Lenny said. "It's time to run again."

The creatures didn't look much like runners, but Desmond knew better than to underestimate them.

The predator in the lead abruptly convulsed, flipping its tail to the side so hard that it slapped its own head. A split second later, it went into the same floundering death roll as the other creature had out in the water.

Without hesitation, the beast coming up behind it tore into its side, ripping its abdomen open and pulling forth a mouthful of entrails. The doomed creature kept spinning, its intestines flopping out and then wrapping around its body as it spun. Soon another of the predators was upon it, and then more came from behind that one. With no sounds other than the tearing of flesh, the scene became another feeding frenzy, this time churning up bloody sand instead of water.

Desmond stopped retreating and turned his eyes to the beings watching from the submarine. One of them flipped a long device to a vertical position, holding the object next to its body as it stared back toward the shore. After watching for several more seconds, the beings began moving toward one end of the watercraft. Their method of locomotion was patently nonhuman, a crab-like motion with their two knees still held at least as high as their heads. One by one, the beings disappeared into a hatch. The last to enter the craft was the individual holding the long device. The being hesitated by the hatch and looked back toward the beach one more time.

Desmond raised a hand above his head, a gesture he hoped would be interpreted as friendly.

The being either didn't notice or chose not to respond. It

handed the device down through the hatch and then climbed through.

The animal-like submarine began moving west. It then arched its ridged back and dove under. Desmond stared as its tail hovered just over the water's surface for a moment before slipping into the depths.

5

———————

ULTIMATUM

MAY 2 - 12:17 PM

INFINITY SHIFTED her gaze from the expanse of ocean where the sub had disappeared to the vicious feeding frenzy still taking place on the beach. She closed her eyes for a moment, urging her heart rate to normalize.

"Hell, now we ain't got but one desalinator," Vic said.

Infinity opened her eyes. She had forgotten she was still clutching her filter. She turned to Desmond. His hands were empty, as were Lenny's and Vic's.

"Don't even recall dropping mine," Lenny said, staring at his hands as if surprised the device was missing.

Infinity shrugged. "Doesn't matter. We won't be trying that again anyway."

Xavier handed them their translators, and they slipped them onto their wrists.

"Do I have to be the first one to say those beings on the submarine just saved our lives?" Desmond asked.

"I watched it happen," Xavier said. "The one guy raised his weapon and pointed it at all of you. I thought he was looking at you through a telescope or something. Then I thought maybe he was going to shoot you. Next thing I know, there's a dead amphibian monster in the water, and you guys are swimming your asses off back to shore. So yeah, I'm pretty sure they saved your lives."

Infinity took another look out at the ocean. Numerous islands dotted the horizon, each only a few miles wide with no more than a mile or so of open water separating it from its neighboring islands. No sign of the whale-submarine. "Maybe," she said. "But they probably just wanted to save us until they figure out what we are. Now that they know we're here, we can expect a visit soon. If they don't like what they see, we might end up like the creatures at the other camp we found. We may have only minutes—or a few hours tops—to prepare a defense."

The others stared at her in silence, contemplating this.

"Hellacious buzz kill," Lenny said.

"She could be right," Desmond countered. "We need to get ready."

Having failed in their mission, and now even thirstier than before, the group left the feeding creatures and began making their way back through the egg-laden swamp.

As they emerged from the inland side of the swamp, Lenny called from behind. "Here's a thought worth considering."

Infinity sighed and turned.

Lenny was carrying what looked like a pile of clear jelly cupped in his hands. He caught up to them and held it out. The jelly was actually three fist-sized whale-salamander eggs. "Hear me out before you dismiss this," he said. "These are eggs. Doesn't matter if they're eggs from a giant mud-groveling, butt-blasting amphibian—they're still eggs. They have a membrane that protects the yolk and embryo." He dropped two of the eggs and began squeezing the third. Globs of the clear stuff started falling away. "If we can rub off this funky jelly, then anything inside has to be relatively free of contaminants, including the yolk and mister wiggle-willy." He wiped away a few more remnants of jelly, resulting in a soft, clear object a little bigger than a chicken egg. The peanut-sized baby inside was now spasming wildly. "The contents of this should be safe to eat."

Xavier shook his head. "The embryo could be toxic. Back home there were innumerable toxic frogs and salamanders."

Lenny pinched the outer membrane and tore it open. He stuck his finger in and flicked the writhing embryo out onto the ground. "I'm way ahead of you, Xavier." He tilted his head back and squirted the yolk into his mouth before anyone could stop him. He raised his brows as he swished it around. Then he swallowed.

"What did it taste like?" Desmond asked.

"Wow, it's actually good! They're obviously high in water content, too." Lenny raised a hand, palm out.

Desmond immediately gave the palm a slap, followed by Vic. Lenny turned the hand toward Xavier.

"You got a kid to raise," Xavier said. "What if—"

"And you got a kid on the way," Lenny interrupted. "You need to keep Celia fat and healthy until she pops the little critter. Salamander eggs, man. That's the answer."

"Okay, it might be a good idea," Infinity said. "But no one else eats those eggs until Lenny goes twenty-four hours without getting sick. Agreed?"

They all nodded.

"Then let's keep moving."

By the time they reached the pile of gear, most of it had already been carried to the new camp site. Armando, Hayley, and Hayley's daughter Isabelle were just arriving at the pile, returning from carrying a load.

After Isabelle assured Lenny that Daisy was being cared for at the new site, he embraced her as if he'd been gone for a week.

When she pulled back with brows raised, he said, "I'll tell you about it on the walk." They both gathered as much as they could carry and took off with Lenny already starting on the story, no doubt adding plenty of extra drama.

Infinity and Desmond, along with Hayley, Xavier, and Vic, picked up the remaining gear, leaving only a few fragments of the broken boxes for Armando to carry.

"We're going to need those," Infinity said. "Can you manage them?"

Armando shot her a look. "I'm old, but I'm not an invalid." He started gathering the fragments.

Infinity glanced at Desmond, who was hanging back waiting for her and Armando, while the others were already steadily moving away. He raised his brows and she nodded.

"Okay, I'm gonna go catch up," he said. "I'll see you two when you get there."

Armando spoke while gathering the last few pieces. "This either means you intend to give me a stern talking-to, or you've got bad news you want to tell me alone."

Infinity almost smiled. "I don't talk sternly to my boss."

"Ha! Is that so?"

"Only when I think I'm right."

He nodded. "So, always?"

This time she actually did smile. "I just want to make sure you're doing okay. Our first few hours here have been a little busy."

"Oh, is that what you call it? Busy? Were all your excursions as *busy* as this?"

She snorted. "Actually, most were much busier."

"Jesus, kiddo! We really didn't pay you bridgers enough, did we?"

"I don't think any of us were in it for the money." She started walking with her load then turned and paused until he caught up. Together they headed southeast, angling toward the hillside.

Infinity said, "Turns out the sea is full of killer monsters. We weren't able to make any fresh water, and we lost all the desalinators but one." She nodded at the last filter pump, which was dangling from her fingers as she carried a five-gallon plastic bag filled with freeze-dried meal packets. "Remind me sometime to tell you that story."

Armando shook his head and muttered something she didn't catch. He was already winded from walking.

A chorus of monkey-frog calls rose in the distance, which was quickly followed by slightly more agitated answering calls. This transformed into enraged crowing calls from both groups, which went on for many seconds. Maybe Reyna had been right—the creatures were simply defending their territories by screaming at each other. Like howler monkeys.

"I heard a few such raucous disputes while you were down at the beach," Armando said. "Those devils are certainly an obstreperous lot."

She glanced over at him. "Just what I was going to say."

They walked in silence for a minute or so.

Finally, Armando said, "You're worried about me, I know. Yes, I could have stayed behind. I had a comfortable life on that world. But all those months—almost two years—I strived to convince the people there to use the Outlanders' instructions, as well as the key tattooed on my back, to construct a fully-functional bridging device. Do you want to know what kept driving me to succeed? It was the belief—the hope—that you were still alive out there somewhere."

"You were just as concerned about the other colonies we bridged out and you know it."

"I'll tell my story the way I want to, kiddo."

She smiled again. "Suit yourself."

"I know I go on like a lonely old man, but you're my family.

And now, thanks to Kitty's procedure, you may even have children someday."

He was lagging behind a bit, so she paused to let him catch up. "Don't count on it. Even if Kitty was telling the truth, it doesn't mean I *should* have a kid. Look at me, Armando. How many scars can you see at this moment, just on this side of my head and body?"

His eyes started darting back and forth as if he were actually trying to count them.

"The point is, too many!" she said. "Do I look like someone who would make a good mother? All I've ever done is fight."

The corners of his mouth turned up a bit. "You'd be a mother grizzly bear. Pity the poor soul who gets between you and your cubs."

Infinity just shook her head.

"I'm not your boss anymore," he said. "I just want to be part of your life. I don't regret my decision to bridge here, and I'll do what I must to carry my own weight and provide wise counsel when needed."

She sighed. "I didn't say you shouldn't be here, but I'm starting to doubt that we'll even live long enough to find out if we're on the right version of Earth."

"Why do you say that?"

She climbed over the jumbled boulders at the east end of the bluff, placed her load on the ground, and extended a hand to help him up. "That whale-machine surfaced again when we were on the beach. Turns out it's a submarine. The creatures that were operating it spotted us."

He climbed over the boulders without her help. "Did you see them? Were they human?"

She hefted the bag of meals back onto her shoulder. "Not even close. At least one of them had a weapon, some kind of rifle, which it used to kill some sea creatures that were about to attack us."

Armando's eyes widened. "That's extraordinary!"

"If you say so." Infinity started walking west along the top of the bluff. "Now that they know we're here, I'm sure they'll be paying us a more personal visit."

He caught up to her. "This is excellent news! We must prepare to greet them properly."

She shot him a glance. "That's the plan."

ONLY NINE OF the original twelve tents had escaped serious damage from the whale-salamander, and those were already set up by the time Infinity and Armando arrived with the final load. Infinity deposited the meal packets with the other supplies and scanned the camp. The tents were erected along the massive boulders that were situated about thirty yards back from the bluff, probably to prevent people from stumbling out in the dark and plunging over the edge. Most of the migrants were busy inspecting and setting up various pieces of equipment such as rain tarps, camp stoves, and sets of lightweight pots, pans, plates, and cooking utensils. Gravity-fed water filters hung from low tree branches, but the dirty-water bags were empty, fluttering gently in the coastal breeze. Various other tools and gadgets were scattered about. Infinity had never been able to bridge with camping gear, so she had no idea how most of the stuff even worked.

Gideon stopped inspecting the shredded tents spread out on the ground and rose to his feet. "I heard your desalination project went to hell. Can't say I'm sorry I missed out on that."

"Did you get the whole story?" Infinity asked.

"About the sub and the beings on it? Yeah." He nodded toward the natural bottleneck of house-sized boulders they had previously discussed. "I've been piling all the empty boxes and fragments over there. I figure there's enough to fashion a fortified barrier on this side. The box material is damn tough, maybe even bullet proof, depending on the weapon."

Infinity shook her head. "We saw them use one of their weapons. The submarine was at least three or four hundred yards out, and the guy nailed a sea creature on the beach with a kill shot."

Gideon grimaced. "Damn. Well, at least they weren't shooting at you."

"Regardless, we need to prepare for a possible conflict. Let's make that bunker our top priority for now."

Gideon nodded once. "You got it."

Armando cleared his throat. "Um, I know you two have more experience with such things, but isn't it possible that preparing for a conflict with these beings might make said conflict a self-fulfilling prophecy?"

Infinity had already headed for the bunker site, but she paused. "Preparing is just preparing. Nothing more."

She started to turn away again, but this time Gideon grabbed her arm. "There's something I'm getting concerned about. Steven, Gibson, and those two wildcard chicks haven't come back."

Infinity turned and scanned the area. "They were just supposed to make spears. They wouldn't have to go far to do that."

Gideon pointed west. "They went off that way when you headed to the beach. Ain't seen them since."

She growled in frustration. "Jesus Christ! How long has it been?"

Gideon was one of the few who had opted to bring a wrist-watch, and he glanced at it. "Almost two hours."

She rubbed her forehead, thinking. "Okay, if they're not back in another hour, we'll deal with it then. For now, our top priority is—"

"Speak of the devil and he doth appear," Armando interjected, nudging Infinity's shoulder. He nodded to the west.

Approaching the camp along the top of the bluff was Gibson, Tessa, and Latonya. Steven was not with them.

Emily Sanchez was the first to speak as the migrants gathered around the returning wildcards. "Where's my husband?"

With grim faces, they dropped about ten sharpened spears into a pile.

Gibson took a deep breath before speaking. "We found a few of these saplings perfect for fashioning spears, so we headed to the west to look for more."

"Where the hell is he?" Emily demanded.

"We spread out to find the saplings. After the three of us got back together we called to him. Nothing. He wasn't supposed to get out of earshot. We searched for an hour with no luck."

Emily rushed forward and attacked the man, punching furiously with both fists and driving him back several steps. "You bastard!" she screamed.

Emily was heavier than Infinity by at least thirty pounds and was a former National Guardsman, but Gibson skillfully deflected her blows. "Stop fighting and listen! I'm telling the truth."

Emily stopped throwing punches. "I knew you people were trouble! What did you do to Steven?"

Infinity stepped forward. It was time to act, but without losing sight of the colony's immediate needs. "Emily's right. You wildcards are trouble, and I want you out of this goddamn colony. All five of you."

"That's not fair, Infinity," said Sue. "Donica and I weren't even—"

"You heard me!"

Gibson narrowed his eyes. "You need us, and we need you. You know that. We didn't do anything to Steven."

"Then go find him! All five of you. If you find him and bring him back safely, you can stay for now. If you don't, then don't bother returning. Ever!"

Gibson continued glaring at her. "What if we only find his body? What if some creature killed him?"

"You better hope that's not the case."

After a few seconds of silence, Gibson nodded. "Fair enough. In fact, that's an admirable strategic move on your part. I can see why the others consider you a leader."

Infinity didn't let up. "I don't want your approval. I want you to get out there and find Steven. You're wasting valuable time."

He gestured to the four women. "Let's get started."

Without saying a word, the women gathered behind him.

"I'm going with them," Emily said. "I don't trust them."

Infinity turned to her. "I don't trust them either, which is why you shouldn't go with them."

"I agree with Infinity," said Desmond.

"So do I," Gideon added.

"We all agree, Emily." said Hayley Millwright. "Don't worry, hon. If these people don't find Steven, we'll all go out together and search for him."

Emily pursed her lips for a moment but then nodded. She turned to the wildcards. "If you people did something to him, I'll hunt you down and kill you all one by one."

"Again, fair enough," Gibson said. He then turned and led his four mates back the way he had come.

6

____

BUNKER

MAY 2 - 3:14 PM

DESMOND SHOOK his head as he watched Vic deftly drill a hole through two adjacent boxes, push a bolt through the two holes, and then thread on a nut. "I didn't even know we'd packed these tools and hardware. Was it your idea?"

Vic glanced over at Desmond, another bolt hanging out from the corner of his mouth. "Heck yeah," he said around the bolt. "I'm kind of a whiz with hand tools, man. When I heard we could bridge inorganic objects, first thing I did was make a list: battery-powered impact drills, reciprocating saws, circular saws, you name it. I got solar chargers for them too, at least those that weren't crushed all to shit."

Desmond stepped back and inspected the barricade Vic had constructed almost single-handedly over the front of the bunker. The Marine had even bolted the corner boxes directly to the boulders. There was one small entrance, only four feet high, which could be defended from the inside by only one or two migrants who were proficient with knives or spears.

Of course, the entire bunker design was based on defense against human-like attackers. It would be much less effective if something could fly in or climb in from the top. There was also the possibility that the creatures he'd seen on the submarine had weapons powerful enough to shoot directly through the boxes.

"I just hope we don't have to test this bunker at all," Desmond said.

"Hope for the best, plan for the worst," Vic replied, still talking around the bolt.

Desmond left him to his work and decided to help Hayley and Alexander Millwright, who were preparing the colony's first meal on their new home world. The couple had become extraordinary chefs during the eighteen months on the arthropod world. They'd invented countless recipes using the meat of giant isopods, hermit crabs, and other bugs, often boiled with various mosses over burning bundles of dried moss. Now they seemed perplexed by the array of compact camping stoves and freeze-dried meal packets spread out on the ground before them.

Rather than bringing the usual white gas or butane back-packing stoves campers often used, which would rely on a limited supply of fuel, the team had opted for specialized stoves designed to concentrate heat from burning bark and twigs. As long as the supply of matches and lighters didn't run out, the stoves would—in theory—last forever. Unfortunately, five of the twelve stoves had been crushed beyond recognition.

Desmond settled onto the ground cross-legged and watched the Millwrights for a few minutes to determine how he could help. It appeared they had successfully lit three of the stoves. Hayley was gingerly feeding twigs into the lit stoves while Alexander was trying to light two more. Beside one of the stoves were two bladders filled with greenish-brown water from the swamp. Even from where he sat several feet away, Desmond could see tiny creatures swimming about in the water.

"You know you're going to have to boil that water a good ten minutes, right?"

Alexander was sitting on his butt with his good leg and prosthetic leg stretched out in front of him. He glanced up, looking a bit frustrated. "We're well aware. Perhaps you'd like to bring us some filtered water?"

"I would if I could," Desmond said. "I'm hoping by tomorrow we'll have a reliable source. You know, we won't starve to death if we wait to have our first meal tomorrow."

Hayley flashed the same smile that had helped her win the presidency before Earth's collapse. "Desmond, you know we're not going to do that. We need to feel useful. We're going to prepare a nourishing meal of," she picked up one of the freeze-dried packets and read the label, "Chili Mac with Beef." She then made a disapproving face.

Desmond leaned over and grabbed another of the packets. Teriyaki Chicken. "We need to boil two cups of water for each of these. Currently there are sixteen of us here, so eight packets. That's sixteen cups of water, exactly a gallon."

"Make that two gallons," Alexander said. "Ten minutes of boiling will reduce it by half."

Desmond sighed. "Crap. This is going to take a while."

Forty minutes later, most of the migrants were seated around a cluster of burning stoves, waiting for the pots of water to finish boiling. Desmond had been scanning the surrounding forest—east, west, uphill, and downhill—for signs of Steven and the wildcards. If Infinity was correct, the beings from the submarine would be somewhere in the area, drawn here by curiosity or perhaps the desire to slaughter the human migrants.

The potential threat made it difficult to relax and anticipate sharing the first meal as a colony. Desmond needed to occupy his mind with other thoughts, so he tore open the first of the eight meal packets the Millwrights had selected. He fished the tiny envelope of desiccant from the contents, set it aside, and situated the food packet upright on the ground, ready to receive boiling water. He repeated this procedure with the seven remaining packets. Finally, he poured about two cups of the now-sterilized greenish-brown water into each packet and closed the zipper seals.

Lenny spoke up. "We'd be eating by now if you'd dumped the yolk from whale-salamander eggs into those pots instead of swamp water. No need to boil for ten minutes."

No one replied. They'd all heard about him swallowing the yolk, and they'd all agreed to avoid the eggs until it was clear Lenny wasn't going to get sick.

Lenny looked at Daisy, who was sitting in his lap. "But no one listens to Daddy, do they? No, of course they don't."

Isabelle patted Lenny's head as if she were comforting a child. "I listen to you, sweetheart."

Emily had been pacing around the perimeter of the camp, but now she plopped down in the circle of migrants. "If Steven doesn't show up by the time we finish eating, I'm going to look for him. By myself if I have to."

Desmond exchanged a glance with Infinity.

"You won't have to go alone," Infinity said. "We'll split up. Half the group will help you search, half will stay here. Sunset is at about 8:00 PM. We'll have about three hours to search. If the wildcards don't find him, we will."

Emily half-smiled, apparently satisfied with this.

Desmond decided the group needed a more engaging conversation. "I'd like to discuss what we know about this version of Earth. Specifically, how long ago it might have diverged from our own."

"This is what we call the nerd talk," Infinity said, apparently for the benefit of Vic, Reyna, and Armando, the only migrants present who hadn't lived with Desmond and the others on the arthropod world.

Reyna laughed at this, and Vic said, "Hey, we're all nerds about something, right? I'd like to hear what the scientists think."

"So far we don't have much to go on, other than the plants and animals we've seen," Desmond offered.

Xavier's face lit up at the chance to speculate. "Let's consider what we know of the plants. The tree species here are unfamiliar to me, but structurally they're similar to the Missouri trees of our own Earth. I saw a few that are probably oaks, just not the species of oaks we know from home. To me this indicates the divergence took place after the origin of the main categories of angiosperm trees. So probably less than 160 million years ago."

"Dude," said Lenny, "you're assuming we're in Missouri."

Xavier frowned. "How can we not be in Missouri? SafeTrek Bridging on our Earth was in Missouri, and the bridging center on the red howler fever version of Earth is in Missouri. Which means we have to be in Missouri here!"

Lenny shook his head. "No go, bro. Just because previous bridging devices sent you to the exact same location on the alternate world, doesn't mean Kitty and her fuzzy-ass compatriots couldn't make a device that can send you to a different *location* on an alternate world." He tapped his forehead. "Remember, Kitty's people have wicked-frosty smarts."

"I don't see how it's possible," Xavier muttered.

Desmond said, "Let's consider the location issue. There are two possibilities. First, we were bridged to another location on an alternate Earth. If that's true, then it shouldn't surprise us that the tree species are unfamiliar. Even on our own Earth they'd be unfamiliar to us in a different part of the world. But I agree with Xavier—I don't think it's possible. Kitty never mentioned anything about this ability. So, for now, I say we go with the second possibility, that we're in Missouri."

"Okay, fine," Lenny said. "Let's look at where we are—beaches and islands and a subtropical climate. A large portion of the midwest United States looked like this about a hundred million years ago, so maybe Xavier's estimate is close. Maybe this world diverged about 160 to 100 million years ago."

Desmond chewed his lip, enjoying this distraction. "That all makes sense, until we consider the animals we've seen so far. I know we haven't been here long, but has anyone seen a single creature that is definitely a reptile, bird, or mammal?"

Everyone in the circle of migrants remained silent.

He held both his hands out, palms up. "Neither have I. But I have seen plenty of creatures that appear to be amphibians, or amphibian-like."

"And a few that were probably fish," Lenny added.

Desmond pointed a finger at Lenny. "Exactly. But no reptiles, no birds, and no mammals."

"So much for a 160-million-year divergence," Xavier said.

Reyna spoke up. "Why does that mean the world couldn't have a 160-million-year divergence?"

"Because," Desmond explained, "Reptiles appeared about 310 million years ago. Mammals arrived 210 million years ago. They would have already become dominant groups by 160 million years ago. Reptiles and mammals were far better adapted to living on land and could outcompete the amphibians for resources."

She seemed genuinely interested. "So you're saying divergence had to be before the reptiles even appeared. You know, because there aren't any reptiles here today."

"You got it," Lenny replied. "It's possible the reptiles could have appeared 310 million years ago and then disappeared after divergence 160 million years ago. But that's wicked unlikely because they were so well established by then." He shook his head. "Wicked unlikely."

Reyna then said, "If this world diverged from ours 160 million years ago, do you think the big asteroid impact would have still occurred 66 million years ago?"

This was followed by several long seconds of silence.

Desmond realized Reyna was making a terrific point. "Yes, the impact probably would have occurred, since there are very few possible events that could have altered the asteroid's course."

Xavier continued the line of thought, "She's suggesting that this world may have diverged 160 million years ago, at which point the reptiles and mammals were well established. And then the—"

Lenny took over. "And then the Chicxulub asteroid struck 66 million years ago, as you would expect it to. But on this particular world it wiped out all the reptiles and mammals."

Reyna said, "Maybe the amphibians survived because they spent more time in the safety of the water."

Vic was now staring at his girlfriend as if he were seeing a side of her he'd never seen. "But what about the birds?" he asked.

Reyna turned to him. "With all the dinosaurs gone, there aren't any birds. On our world they evolved from the surviving avian dinosaurs several million years after the asteroid impact."

"Hot damn, Reyna!" Lenny said. "You didn't tell us you had a background in evolutionary history."

She blushed and looked at her feet. "I just used to watch some TV. You know, those nature shows."

"Sounds like you've figured it all out," Infinity said. "If the nerd talk is over, someone open those meals so we can eat."

Desmond opened the nearest packet, which was still hot, and gazed inside. The contents were supposed to be Pad Thai Veggies. He frowned and passed the packet to Lenny. "Here, you and Xavier can share this one."

"Incoming!" Infinity said abruptly. She leapt to her feet, staring to the west.

Desmond turned. Several figures were running toward camp along the top of the bluff.

"It's Steven!" Emily cried. She jumped up and ran.

Everyone got up and rushed to the edge of camp. Steven was running in the lead, with all five wildcards just behind. For a moment, Desmond thought the wildcards were chasing him, but then Steven embraced Emily and the wildcards whisked by him and came to a stop before the rest of the migrants.

"We found him about a mile to the west," Tessa panted. "He's fine."

"But we've got visitors coming this way," Gibson said. "They're sentient beings, without a doubt. I've never seen anything like them. They looked to be well armed, and they're riding on the backs of some kind of domesticated creatures."

Steven and Emily stepped up beside Gibson. "We ran to get ahead of them," Steven said. "They may have seen us—I don't know. But we've got only seconds before they get here."

"The spears and knives are in the bunker," Infinity said without hesitating. "Move it, people. Now!"

"Go!" Desmond said as the migrants rushed past him toward the bunker.

The wildcards stood in place, watching.

Desmond glanced at Infinity, his brows raised.

She nodded and turned to Gibson. "You guys too. Get in the bunker."

Once the migrants, including the wildcards, had ducked single file into the bunker, Infinity paused by the opening, waiting for Desmond to enter.

"Go on," he said. "I'm staying out here."

"The hell you are. Get in."

He shook his head. "I'm still assuming Kitty sent us here to meet these beings. Someone's got to stay out here and talk to them." He nodded toward his wrist. "I've got my translator. And we both know I'm better suited to diplomacy than you are."

Her jaw muscles rippled as she stared at him.

"You know I'm right," he said. Then a movement over her shoulder caught his eye. He squinted. Several massive creatures were approaching from the west, lumbering along atop the bluff, with even more coming into view from the forest behind them. Mounted on each creature's back was a being with two long legs folded up at its sides, the knees situated higher than the top of the being's head—the beings from the submarine. Each of them held a long, black object vertically at its side.

Infinity swung around and stared at the approaching party. "Those aren't peace pipes they're carrying, Desmond. We need to get in the bunker."

He didn't move. "*You* get in the bunker. I'm going to try to talk to them."

"Shit!" she said and ducked into the opening. Two seconds later she emerged with one of the spears and stood at his side. "What if they don't want to talk? What if the translator takes too long to learn their language? What if they don't even *have* a goddamn language?"

He turned to her and forced a smile. "Relax. Let's just see what happens, okay?"

She let out a growl, gripping the spear with white knuckles.

Desmond turned back to the approaching beings. Although their mounts walked on four legs rather than hopping, they were frog-like, with broad mouths and thicker hindlegs than forelegs. Their hairless skin was a rusty-brown color except for the tops of their heads and backs, which were dark orange. Loose skin beneath their chins jiggled back and forth with each step, and Desmond envisioned the creatures inflating their chins to the size of beach-balls when producing their mating calls.

These frog-like steeds appeared to weigh at least eight hundred pounds each. They were certainly striking in appearance, but they were of a typical terrestrial quadruped form. Their riders, on the other hand, were like no Earth creatures Desmond had ever seen. They were now close enough for him to make out details. When he had observed them on the submarine, he'd been uncertain whether their long, folded limbs were legs or arms. Now he was no more certain than before. There was definitely another pair of smaller limbs, but these seemed to originate at the same points of attachment as the long limbs—just below the shoulders. Below the attachment points of the four limbs, the torso appeared actually to be the base of a thick tail. About three feet below the shoulders, this tail split into two tails, both of which hung loosely over one side of the horse-frog mount.

The beings continued approaching without making a sound, and now Desmond could clearly see their faces. At first he thought they had foot-long tusks, but these turned out to be ornaments hanging loosely from rings piercing the loose skin on either side of the face. Thick, fleshy ridges ran vertically from chin to forehead on the left and on the right side, just in front of the two ornaments. These ridges were adorned with dozens of white, circular rings piercing the flesh.

Desmond's gaze was ultimately drawn to the beings' eyes. Each of them had two pairs of eyes, one pair arranged about three inches higher on the face than the other pair. The four eyes were each about an inch in diameter and were almost perfectly round, apparently lacking lids that could blink. Desmond stared at their eyes as the beings came to a stop ten yards away. Their pupils were neither round nor vertical. Instead, they projected out from the center in three directions, like black, three-pointed stars.

In the center of each face, above the bottom pair of eyes and below the top pair, was a red, dangly protrusion, reminding Desmond of the snood on a male turkey. Several inches below the lower pair of eyes was a round, anus-like hole, perhaps the mouth. Every second or two, the muscles around this hole contracted, opening the hole to about two inches in diameter, either to inhale, exhale, or both.

Infinity nudged him. "You gonna say something or just stare?"

Desmond snapped out of his hypnotic trance. The beings, eight of them in total, were now sitting motionless on their steeds, gazing at him and Infinity. One of them shifted its four eyes up and down, apparently appraising the bunker. So far, they hadn't raised their weapons toward the humans.

Desmond held up a hand, palm out. "We've come here as friends. We don't mean you any insult or harm."

He had expected his translator would need to hear several minutes of the beings speaking—assuming they could speak at all— before his translator could begin to try interpreting. So he was surprised when the device immediately responded. It spat out a series of clicks and buzzes, sounding more like plastic and metal objects being rubbed together than any spoken language.

Almost simultaneously, the beings' shoulders changed shape. A small arm-like appendage unfolded on either side of their heads. The appendages, each about fourteen inches long, were jointed at about the midpoint, and the portion beyond the joint looked like a hairless, prehensile opossum's tail. Each of these appendages moved purposefully, first wiping the membrane covering the top eye on that side of the head and then wiping the bottom eye. This all happened within about three seconds, then the appendages returned to their original positions tucked against each shoulder.

"What the hell are these guys?" Infinity muttered.

Fortunately, their translators recognized that she wasn't speaking to the beings and didn't interpret this.

One of the beings began moving its smaller pair of arms, somehow producing those same types of clicks and buzzes from somewhere in the area of its armpits. After about thirty seconds of this, it held its arms still and fell silent.

Desmond's translator interpreted in perfect English. "We do not believe you. We believe you have come here to kill us."

The eight beings turned their weapons in unison and leveled them at Desmond and Infinity.

7

CONTACT

MAY 2 - 4:50 PM

INFINITY GRIPPED HER SPEAR, though with eight weapons pointed at her it seemed useless. Her fears had been warranted—these beings had come to kill her and the other migrants, just like they'd killed the human-like creatures at the other camp.

She muttered to Desmond the only option she could think of. "When I step in front of you, duck into the bunker—fast. I'll take one of them out. That'll confuse them long enough for me to duck in right behind you."

"No," he replied. "We have to reason with them." He then smiled at the beings who were pointing their rifles at him. "We have not come here to threaten or harm you. Please put away your weapons so we may talk."

His translator promptly interpreted his words by creating a series of sounds like several grasshoppers clicking and buzzing at the same time.

The nearest of the beings replied by moving his two small arms.

Desmond's translator said, "We do not believe you. We want you to go back to where you came from."

"We cannot go back," Desmond explained. "This world is our new home. Please do not hurt us. We want to be your friends."

This was translated, and again the being spoke by moving his arms. "Why can you not go back?"

"We do not have the technology needed to go back. We have come here to live the rest of our lives."

One of the other beings somehow commanded the creature beneath him to move forward a few steps. He pointed his weapon at Desmond's face, holding the gun with one of his ridiculously-long arms. He then pumped his two smaller arms to speak. Desmond's translator said, "You have come here for retribution. If we do not stop you now, you will return to where you came from, and you will come back with more of your kind to kill all of us."

As the translation ended, another of the beings spoke, and Desmond's translator interpreted. "You will kill all of us, and then you and others like you will occupy our city."

Another one followed with, "You will not understand the workings and the purpose of our city. Our city will then begin to fail."

Yet another spoke. "And you will not understand the symbolic importance of the design of our dwellings and ornamentations. Our heritage will become merely an unimportant annoyance to you and your kind."

"And you will neglect our cultivated livestock," another said. "Our revered creatures will languish and die due to your failure to understand their care and their importance."

"When our city begins to sag due to your neglect, and when our revered livestock begin to die, you and your kind will begin to modify our city to suit your own whims."

"You will create dwellings with little resemblance to ours, and your ornamentations will suit you but will reflect little of our culture."

As yet another of the beings began speaking, Infinity nudged Desmond. "What the hell is happening?"

His eyes flicked in her direction. "I have no idea."

The being finished its statement, and Desmond's translator continued interpreting the increasingly bizarre words. "Our memory will fade in your minds, and a day will come when no trace of our existence can be found on this world."

As another of the beings began flexing his noise-producing arms, Infinity took a half step forward and raised her free hand. "Um, I want to say something."

As her translator spoke, the being stopped moving its arms and the entire group sat on their frog-steeds gazing at her—eight beings, two pairs of eyes each. Even the ugly steeds were now staring.

"We didn't come here to kill you," she said. "And we don't want to occupy your city or do anything to your livestock. We want to be your friends."

After listening to the translation, one of the beings said, "Why can you not go back to where you came from?"

Infinity glanced at Desmond, but he just frowned. She turned back to the beings. "He just told you. We don't have the technology to go back."

"Tell us about where you came from."

Desmond took over. "It's another version of this world. That world is much like this world but with different animals and plants. Before that, most of us lived on yet another version of this world. Unfortunately, that world no longer exists."

The beings listened. Just as the clicking translation ended, their behavior abruptly changed. While talking, the beings had relaxed their weapons, allowing the rifles to point down at the ground, but now they snapped the guns back up menacingly. Several of the beings began speaking rapidly.

"Get in the goddamn bunker!" Infinity ordered. She dropped her spear and charged the nearest being. She reached for his rifle, intending to pull him from his mount and use his body as a shield, hoping the others would be reluctant to sacrifice one of their own to kill her.

Before she even reached the rifle, the being's frog-steed lunged forward and clamped its wide mouth onto her arm. The creature bit down, puncturing her skin and threatening to crush the bones of her forearm. All eight guns were now pointed at her head.

"Stop, please!" Desmond cried as he threw himself in front of Infinity, blocking her from at least a few of the weapons.

"We're coming out!" Gideon shouted from within the bunker.

Infinity saw movement at the entrance. "Stay there, Gideon!" she cried, knowing in her gut that if the others came pouring out, this situation would become a massacre. The shredded tents and bleached bones of the other colony flashed through her mind. "All of you stay in there!"

One of the beings clicked and buzzed. "You want to kill us. We will not let you kill us."

Still standing between Infinity and the weapons, Desmond said, "Please don't shoot. We were sent here by some other beings, and we think you may know them. They look like us, only with black fur on their bodies." He motioned to his head and torso. "Black fur all over. They sent us here! They said you would *not* be a threat to us. They said you would benefit from having us here with you. And on the beach earlier today you helped us. You killed the aquatic animals that were attacking us. You don't really want to kill us, do you?"

The beings remained motionless as they listened to the translation. Infinity tried pulling her arm loose, but the frog-steed clamped down ever harder. Her blood was starting to ooze out beneath its lips.

One of them again cranked its arms up and down to speak. "Tell us more about these other beings," Desmond's translator said.

"They have black fur, and they decorate the fur with colored dyes in certain patterns." Desmond held his wrist up. "They gave us these language translators so we could communicate with you. These beings are technologically advanced, at least compared to us. They can bridge from world to world in ways that we have never been able to. They said you would *not* be a threat to us."

After listening to the translation, the eight beings began clicking and buzzing to each other. The translators didn't respond. Finally, one of the beings turned to Infinity and Desmond.

"Yes, we know of these beings. They haven't come here in a long time, long before any of us were birthed. But we have stories about them from previous generations. They created us and put us on this world. We are grateful to them for that. If they created you and put you on this world, then you have not come here to kill us. Therefore, we should not kill you." They lowered their weapons in unison.

The rider Infinity had tried to attack lifted one of his smaller, three-fingered hands and tapped his steed's head. The creature released her arm. She rubbed the blood away and inspected the wounds. Nothing serious, unless the damn thing's saliva contained nasty microbes. Which it probably did.

The beings sat there watching the humans, waiting for some kind of response.

Desmond put a hand on his chest. "Thank you. We will not try to harm you if you do not try to harm us. We would like to be friends."

One of the beings turned as if scanning the area. "Where are the black-fur beings? After they created you, did they not stay and teach you what you must know to live here?"

Infinity was still rubbing her arm. "Those beings didn't create us. They just sent us here to live our lives in peace. And no, they didn't come with us."

The beings remained silent for a moment after listening to the translation. Finally, one of them spoke. "The black-fur beings sent you here but did not create you. You must know very much, or the black-fur beings would have stayed here to teach you as they taught us."

Another of the beings added, "Perhaps you know more than the black-fur beings know, and that is why they did not teach you."

Another one said, "You know more than the black-fur beings, and so they must have sent you here to teach us what you know."

And another said, "You will teach us, and then we will know more than the black-fur beings. We will then improve our city. We will create better dwellings and better water vehicles."

The one who had first asked about Kitty's people said, "But then our city, and our dwellings, and our vehicles will begin to transform. They eventually will reflect your tastes and knowledge, and our culture will become lost over time."

Infinity started to say something but then just shut her mouth. What the hell was wrong with these beings?

Desmond apparently couldn't help himself. "It seems to me that you are jumping to conclusions. We definitely aren't smarter than the people who sent us here—the black-fur beings. They are far more technologically advanced than we are. And I really don't know if we have much to offer regarding your city and your vehicles."

Again there was a pause. Infinity found it disturbing to stare at creatures who were staring at her with four eyes each.

One of the beings said, "The black-fur beings must have sent you here to help us defeat those who will come here to kill us. There will surely be others who come to kill us."

Another said, "Yes, the black-fur beings must know that others will come here for retribution. You will help us defeat them."

And another, "Together we must begin preparing."

Desmond turned around to face Infinity with a baffled expression. He shook his head before turning back to the beings. "Again, I think you're making assumptions that aren't... well, we didn't really come here to help you fight attackers. If we become friends, we will certainly help you in ways that we can. Perhaps we should get to know each other better first, and then—gradually—maybe we'll find out how we can assist each other. What do you think of that?"

Once again, a pause. The immediate threat appeared to be over, so Infinity allowed herself to relax a little. It seemed she had been wrong—this was the very world Kitty had promised her after all. Infinity had first suspected it when she realized the translators already knew the beings' click-and-buzz language. And then the beings had said that Kitty's people had created them and had taught them. Whatever that meant.

"We think that we agree with you," said one of the beings.

Another one added, "Yes, we agree. We should get to know each other first. Some of us will now return to our city. I and two others will stay here with you. We will observe you and speak with you. We will get to know each other."

Five of the beings swung their mounts around and headed back to the west without further discussion. The remaining three sat motionless, gazing at Infinity and Desmond with unblinking eyes and three-pronged pupils.

8

____

INTERACTION

MAY 2 - 5:39 PM

"WE WERE JUST GETTING ready to eat a meal," Desmond said, for lack of anything better to say. "Would you like to join us? You're welcome to have some of our food."

The three beings continued staring, perhaps processing this invitation.

"Should we come out now?" Gideon called from within the bunker.

"Do it nice and slow," Infinity replied.

Desmond spoke to the beings. "There are twenty-two of us here. The others are coming out now, so don't be alarmed."

Gideon appeared first, followed by Armando, who took one look at the beings and said, "Extraordinary!"

Soon all the migrants were standing outside of the bunker, ogling their guests. Desmond couldn't blame them. He felt mesmerized by the utterly alien nature of these beings. He couldn't think of a single scenario that even came close to explaining how such creatures could evolve from any of the animals that had ever lived on Earth.

"Wicked freakin' awesome!" Lenny exclaimed. He then addressed the beings. "I'd like to personally welcome you to our camp. It's not much to look at because, well, we just got here."

The three beings listened to the clicks and buzzes from Lenny's translator and then abruptly slid off their frog-steeds, causing Desmond and some of the other migrants to step back in surprise. The beings landed on their two long legs, which bent at the knees, causing their bodies to sink down until the bases of their tails were only a few inches above the ground. Their knees stood five feet high, a foot higher than their heads, while their long, two-pronged tails were curled snugly around their waists. Each being's waist appeared also to be the base of its tail, so it was more like the two tail ends were wrapped around the thicker portion of the tail itself. Desmond noticed that each being was wearing a black pouch— almost like a fannypack—around the thick base of its tail just below the attachment points of the two long legs and two short arms. He couldn't discern any physical features that might be sexual organs. The beings' two smaller limbs, a bit shorter than human arms and having only three fingers, still gripped the rifle-like weapons, but these were now pointed harmlessly at the sky.

One of the beings turned to face its steed. Balancing on one folded leg, it lifted and extended its other leg until its foot—or hand —was resting on the crown of the steed's head. Like the smaller hands, this hand had three jointed fingers, but these fingers were much longer, at least ten inches each. The fingers caressed the crea- ture's head for a moment. Then the being drew back its hand and smacked the animal on top of its head. The creature let out a burp- like grunt and took off running to the west. The other two beings did the same with their mounts, and soon the three frog-steeds had disappeared among the trees at the far end of the rocky bluff.

The beings turned back to face the migrants. Desmond realized their hairless, unclothed skin was gradually changing color. He thought the beings were uniformly brownish-gray before. Now that they were off their steeds and standing on the ground they seemed to have more of a greenish tint, and their overall shade was getting darker.

"What do you call those animals you were riding?" Desmond asked after a period of awkward silence.

After the translation, one of the beings pumped its small arms while still holding its rifle. "Such names are not likely to be translated well by that device on your arm. If you wish the animals to have a name, you will have to create the name yourself."

Desmond considered this. "So, if I tell you my name is Desmond, does my translator give you a name that makes any sense?"

His translator spat out a series of buzzes and clicks.

The being replied, and Desmond's translator said, "As expected, the device on your arm translated your name as *identity designation*. Therefore it is likely to do the same for you when I tell you that my name is... *identity designation*."

Armando spoke up. "Well, then, we'll come up with names for you based upon characteristics we learn about you." He pointed to the being who had been speaking. "You, for instance. What is something you would like to tell us about yourself?"

The being's shoulders unfolded and the two prehensile, finger-like appendages whipped out and wiped its upper eyes and then its lower eyes before folding back onto its shoulders. Desmond heard several of the migrants mutter hushed expressions of surprise.

The creature then pumped its arms to speak, and Armando's translator said, "I am particularly skilled at harvesting creatures from the water of the sea. In this way I contribute to the well-being of the population of my city."

After the translation, Armando rubbed his hands together.

"Excellent. Then we shall call you Fisher. Would that be okay with you?"

Fisher listened to the translation and then simply stared back without answering.

"I'll take that as a yes," Armando said. He then asked the same question of the next being, who said that he—or she—was also adept at harvesting aquatic game. When Armando explained that more information would be helpful in order to choose a different name, the being went on to reveal that he had once almost been killed by the same kind of aquatic predators that had attacked Desmond, Infinity, Lenny, and Vic earlier in the day. In fact, this individual confessed that he was the one who had shot and killed two of the predators, thus saving the humans from being torn to bite-sized shreds. Armando gave him the name Hero.

Without being asked, the third being explained that he contributed to the well-being of his people by speaking. Armando pushed for clarification, and after several exchanges it became clear the being was some kind of storyteller, although the purpose of this was still unclear. Desmond supposed maybe it was a form of entertainment, or perhaps a way of teaching others. Armando announced this being's name would be Bard.

Fisher, Hero, and Bard. Easy enough to remember, although Desmond hadn't noticed any particular physical characteristics that would help him distinguish between the three. They looked to him like three copies of the same alien creature. As he looked closer, though, he did notice the ornamental tusks hanging from the bulgy flesh of Bard's face were only half the length of those worn by Fisher and Hero. Also, close to fifty white rings pierced the flesh on either side of Fisher's and Bard's faces, while no more than twenty adorned either side of Hero's.

Fisher began clicking and buzzing, and Desmond assumed the being was initiating the process of naming the humans, but then his translator said, "You told us that you would share your food with us, but you have not given us any food."

Desmond blinked. "Oh, yeah. Sorry about that. Over here." He began backing toward the cluster of camp stoves and rehydrated meal packets, gesturing for Fisher, Hero, and Bard to follow.

With their knees still positioned higher than their heads, they shuffled after him, walking sideways instead of forward, like giant, two-legged fiddler crabs. The migrants followed, most of them cautiously keeping their distance.

Desmond picked up one of the food packets, which was now only lukewarm. He pulled apart the zipper seal, releasing a reasonably pleasant aroma.

Hayley stepped forward and held out three titanium sporks to the beings. "These are eating utensils."

Fisher extended one of his small arms and deftly plucked the sporks from her hand. He then held out his rifle to her and somehow managed to move his two arms to generate the sounds of his language. Hayley's translator interpreted. "We do not wish to hold these in our possession at this time."

Hayley hesitated only briefly before accepting the weapon.

Hero and Bard handed her their weapons as well. Bard said, "You should be cautious with those. If you use them to kill us, you will be unable to get to know us, then the others from our city will come and kill you."

Hayley's eyes widened and she turned to the other migrants. "Can somebody, um... I really don't want to handle these."

Gideon, Emily, and Steven stepped up, and each of them carefully took one of the weapons. Desmond took a good look at the weapons for the first time. Although they had proven to be extremely accurate at the beach, the devices appeared to be little more than black tubes, each with a sight at both ends and an odd-shaped stock. The stocks, also black, featured several holes and bumps, but nothing that looked like the triggers on almost all human-made firearms.

Desmond picked up a bowl from the dishes stacked on the ground and dumped in about half of the food packet's teriyaki chicken. He felt ridiculous offering such food. For all he knew, it might poison them, but there was no turning back now. He held out the bowl to Fisher.

Fisher's left shoulder shuddered slightly and its short limb unfolded. He lifted the spork higher, and the flexible tentacle at the end of his shoulder limb wrapped around the utensil and plucked it from his fingers. He took the bowl from Desmond and—ignoring the spork—dipped a finger into the food. He contracted the muscles surrounding his mouth, opening it to a perfectly round, two-inch hole, and stuck the food-covered finger inside. The orifice closed on his finger, and he pulled the finger out, leaving the food inside.

Fisher's face muscles contracted in a more or less circular fashion, which looked nothing like a typical lower jaw chewing up and down. The motion made Desmond think of the circular mouth of a sea lamprey. These beings apparently had no lower jaw at all.

Seconds later, Fisher pumped his arms to speak. Desmond's translator said, "This food is not suitable to the needs of my body, and I will not eat any more of it." He handed the bowl back to Desmond then grabbed the spork from his shoulder limb and handed that over too. He spoke again. "I am hungry. I will go and harvest some game animals from the water. Then I will show you how we prepare the food. Perhaps this will help you. Perhaps the food we prepare will be suitable to the needs of your bodies. In this way, we will get to know you, and you will get to know us."

Fisher crab-walked over to Emily and took his gun back. Gripping the weapon with his short arms, he straightened his much longer legs, rising to his full height. Again, several migrants gasped in surprise. Although Fisher's body probably weighed less than two hundred pounds, he was now standing with his head ten feet above the ground. He launched himself over the edge of the rocky bluff and landed lightly on his feet fifteen feet below. He then lumbered off toward the beach at a steady clip.

"Why do they even bother riding those big ugly frogs?" Infinity said, as the group watched Fisher recede into the forest.

Bard stepped up to Desmond, stuck his finger into the bowl of teriyaki chicken, and duplicated Fisher's tasting routine. He spoke. "I agree. This food is not suitable. Do you not have other food?"

Desmond waited, but apparently no one else wanted to answer this, so he said, "We normally eat other foods, but these packets are light, and we could only bring a limited amount of supplies with us."

"Your food is not suitable," Bard said again. "If this is all the food you have, you must surely wish to learn from us how to procure suitable food."

Hero added, "You must surely desire to discard all of your unsuitable food and learn from us."

Bard said, "If you discard all of your food here, you will be discarding your food near the eggs of the... *creature designation*... and the young...*creature designation*...will find the food, and they will eat it."

Hero followed this with, "This will make the young...*creature designation*...change their behavior. If their behavior changes, this will affect the balance of life and death in the sea."

Bard began to say something, but Desmond held up a hand before this line of thought took yet another step into the bizarre. "Please, uh, I think you are again jumping to conclusions. We do not intend to discard our supply of food. And if we decide to, we will be happy to bury it where it will not be found."

"I have a question," Infinity said when Desmond's translator had finished buzzing and clicking. "We found the remains of another camp near here. The people there were similar to us, but they had been killed. Did you kill them?"

Bard and Hero gazed at her as they listened to the translation. Hero replied, "Yes, we killed some of them, but not all of them. I will explain. We saw that those people were here, just as we saw that you were here. We were suspicious of their purpose, so some of us came to investigate. Those people had translators like your translators. We talked to the people. They were kind to us at first, but it turned out that they were not kind people."

Everyone remained silent for a few seconds after the translation had ended.

"What made you think they weren't kind?" Infinity asked.

"They began to kill each other. Those that killed some of the others then tried to kill us. We did not want to be killed."

Infinity glanced at Desmond, frowning, before asking, "Why would they try to kill you?"

Hero and Bard listened to the translation and then stared at her without answering.

Desmond asked, "Were those people sent here by the same beings who sent us here? The ones with black fur all over their bodies?"

"We do not know," Hero replied. "But we assume that they were not. We do not believe that the black-fur beings would send people here who would want to kill us. After all, the black-fur beings created us and taught us how to live here. They left us a production factory so that we could make the components we need to construct our city, our vehicles, and other important devices, including our weapons. When you said that you were sent here by the black-fur beings, we decided that you did not come here to kill us."

"We definitely did not come to hurt you," Infinity said. "You can trust us."

Again, the two beings just stared back at her.

Lenny let out an exaggerated sigh. "Well, some of us are getting damn hungry." He went over and picked up one of the food packets. "And these meals are just sitting here getting cold." He grabbed a spork, sat on the ground, and motioned for Isabelle and Daisy to sit beside him. He took one bite, nodded his approval, and began shoveling the stuff into Daisy's mouth. Daisy flapped her arms up and down, apparently excited to finally eat.

Except for Desmond and Infinity, the rest of the migrants gathered around the remaining food packets.

For at least a full, awkward minute, Bard and Hero stared at Desmond and Infinity without speaking. Abruptly, Bard stepped over to Hero, and the two beings leaned in as if they were going to kiss. As they drew closer, the red snoods situated between their upper and lower pairs of eyes suddenly went from hanging loosely on their faces to projecting outward. Their faces touched, and the two snoods intertwined. The two beings remained this way for a few seconds then pulled away and went back to staring at Desmond and Infinity.

Desmond was tempted to ask about the purpose of this behavior but decided such a question might be considered rude. Instead he said, "We are pleased that you want to get to know us. I'm not sure how long you would like to stay, but is there some way we can make you more comfortable?"

Bard spoke, and Desmond's translator said, "We will stay until we know what our next course of action should be."

Desmond exchanged a puzzled look with Infinity then said, "If you think you might spend the night here, we have shelters." He waved his hand at the array of nine tents. "You could use one of those." He had no idea if these beings even slept at night, but offering them a tent seemed like the polite thing to do. He had doubts, however, as to whether the tents would be large enough if the beings needed to stretch out their gangly legs.

After turning and looking at the tents, Hero said, "Yes, we will spend the night here. But we will construct our own shelter. We will do so now."

Hero and Bard crab-walked to the west end of the camp, with Desmond and Infinity following. The beings scanned the ground and the surrounding area briefly then spoke to each other. The humans' translators didn't interpret this exchange. Both beings unwrapped their dual tails and began using their two small arms and their two prehensile tails to gather sticks and twigs.

Desmond watched in wonder as their movements became a blur of motion. Two beings, each using four limbs simultaneously, plucked sticks from the ground and tossed them into a steadily growing pile. Hero and Bard cleared the ground within a ten-yard radius then moved outward, expanding the circle. Once they were too far out to easily toss the sticks to the center of the area, they started making trips back to the pile. Within only a few minutes, the pile had grown to over a foot deep.

Hero and Bard scuttled to a tree about forty yards to the west. They each rose to their full height, stood on one long leg, and lifted the other leg into the branches of the tree, in this way reaching up more than fifteen feet into the lower branches. They pulled themselves up, apparently with little effort. Seconds later, cracking and tearing sounds were heard as limbs and clusters of leaves began raining down. The beings leapt lightly from the tree and gathered some of the detached limbs and leaf clusters. They quickly made three trips to the pile with their fresh supplies.

Apparently satisfied with their collection of raw materials, Hero and Bard began construction. Armando, Xavier, and several of the other migrants came over to watch the process. As if their stick-gathering skills weren't impressive enough, the beings now displayed a level of skill and efficiency Desmond never imagined possible. The beings pulled several tools from the pouches fastened around their waists. While standing on only one foot, they each began gathering and working with the twigs and larger sticks so fast that it was impossible to discern exactly what they were doing.

Desmond realized that each being was rapidly manipulating

the tools and raw materials with seven different limbs at the same time. Standing on one foot allowed them to use the other foot to hold larger sticks in place. The two prehensile tail ends, acting independently of each other, were gathering more from the pile. The two short shoulder extremities had unfolded and were grasping smaller twigs, and each of the two short arms wielded a tool, whittling, chopping, and splitting the pieces held by all the other limbs.

Amidst flying wood chips and the cracking and cutting sounds from the tools, a domed shelter of woven twigs supported by a framework of thicker sticks began to take shape. Within only a few minutes the structure was almost complete. Abruptly the beings stopped. They talked back and forth, a conversation the humans' translators ignored, then they resumed working. Now they were removing sticks from one side of the structure. Once they'd cleared that side, they started extending the side out until the structure became an odd T shape.

Hero and Bard scuttled back to the tree and returned with the freshly-cut clusters of green leaves.

Again, with unnatural skill and speed, they spliced the leaves into the structure's surface, overlapping them in shingle-like fashion, until the entire structure was covered and appeared to be impervious to wind and rain.

Hero and Bard finally stood back and paused, apparently appraising their handiwork. The main portion of the dwelling was about five feet high, twelve feet long, and eight feet wide. The last-minute addition, that strange offshoot on one side, came out about six feet.

"These creatures are beyond magnificent!" Armando exclaimed. "I do believe they constructed this shelter in less than twenty minutes. I'm afraid that a human brain would be entirely incapable of processing so many simultaneous tasks, not to mention that we are limited to only two hands."

The two beings turned to watch Armando as he spoke, but his translator recognized that he hadn't been directly addressing them and remained silent.

Bard spoke, and Armando's translator interpreted. "Your language is very slow, and it involves patterns I am beginning to identify. I believe that soon I will be able to understand you. But I will never be able to make such strange sounds, so I will never be able to speak to you in your language."

"Well, I am quite certain we cannot produce the sounds of your language," Armando replied. "Perhaps if we can learn to understand it, and if you can learn to understand ours, someday we might speak directly to each other using our own languages." He held up his wrist, displaying the translator. "These are obviously powered devices, and without access to their source of power, they will eventually cease to function."

Desmond hadn't thought of this before, but it made sense. Kitty's people were obviously technologically advanced, but he had a hard time imagining that they could make such a powerful and small computing device without a limit to battery life. Then again, as far as he knew, the devices were self-charging, perhaps aided by movement or sunlight. Or maybe they used a source of power humans hadn't even imagined.

Bard and Hero had gone back to their original body stances, with their knees held above their heads, shoulder limbs folded, and tails wrapped around their waists. Bard was staring down the hillside toward the beach, and he abruptly pointed with one of his small arms and spoke. Armando's translator said, "*Identity designation* now returns with harvested aquatic game."

Everyone turned. Sure enough, Fisher was just approaching the base of the rocky bluff, and he was dragging something behind him.

Fisher easily climbed up the bluff, hauling his catch with him. He crouched and then crab-walked to the center of camp. As the humans gathered around, Fisher handed his weapon to Hayley then dropped the items he'd been holding against his waist—the three lost desalinators, their tubes and bladders still attached. Fisher spoke and Desmond's translator said, "I believe these devices must belong to you."

Desmond glanced at the filter pumps, then his eyes were drawn to the creatures Fisher had caught, which were strung on a thin, black cord. At least fifteen animals lay bleeding on the ground, some of them still moving. Four were obviously fish. Three of the fish were shark-like with smooth skin, and the fourth was covered in thumbnail-sized scales. The rest of the creatures were not so easy to recognize. Most of them had legs, with a basic body structure similar to the much larger crocodile-salamanders that had attacked Desmond's group earlier. He assumed they were amphibians, or perhaps part of a new group that had evolved from amphibians on this world.

Fisher's anus-like mouth opened and closed every second or so, apparently to draw in sufficient air to compensate for the exertion. His skin still glistened with a film of saltwater, and his lower legs were covered in slime and mud from walking through the swamp.

He extended one of his long legs and used his dexterous toes to shove several of the flopping creatures into a heap with the others, and then he pumped his arms to speak. Desmond's translator interpreted. "Now we will help you get to know us by showing you how we prepare suitable food."

9

TEACHING

INFINITY CAREFULLY WATCHED Steven's eyes as the former guardsman told his story. She had lived with him for nearly two years on the arthropod world, and she would trust him with her life, but she didn't trust the wildcards—not yet. She had no idea what kind of influence they may have had on him.

"We split up," Steven said. "I knew we were supposed to stay close, but then I found a stream that dumped into the swamp. I called out to Gibson and the others, but when I didn't get a response, I decided to follow the stream uphill for a little while. Thought maybe I'd find cleaner water farther from the swamp. Turns out I did find good water, but then I got distracted by a pack of animals—at least eight of them, the size of deer. Thought maybe they'd be a good food source. Next thing I know, I get turned around, can't find the stream. I'm a damn idiot."

He seemed sincere, and he hadn't even glanced at Gibson once.

Emily gave Steven's shoulder a playful shove. "Yeah, you're an idiot. Scared the crap out of me." She turned to Gibson and his four mates, who were sitting on the ground to the side. "I owe you guys an apology."

Gibson nodded. "Rough time for all of us. We'll find our rhythm as a team."

Infinity turned to watch Fisher, Hero, and Bard, who were using their multiple extremities and several tools to make quick work of cleaning Fisher's catch. Most of the migrants were gathered around, obviously fascinated by the process.

She turned back to Gibson and his mates. "You know you'll have to tell everyone else what you told us—about your background. That's not a secret you can keep in this colony."

"We're not ashamed of who we are," Tessa said without any indication of anger.

Emily said, "Uh, what are we talking about here?"

Gibson glanced over at the rest of the migrants. "We'll explain the whole thing when everyone is together."

"I have one question I'd like you to answer now," Infinity said. "Why did you leave your cult to join this colony?"

"Are you trying to antagonize us by using that word?" Tessa asked, this time with an edge to her voice.

Infinity ignored her and continued eyeing Gibson.

He gave her a curt nod. "Okay. We left for a few reasons. First, because no one else wanted to join you. It's not like the National Bridging Center wasn't trying to recruit migrants, but everyone else was too frightened to volunteer. They think the United States is now a safe place and assume red howler fever won't ever rear its ugly head again. Maybe it won't, I don't know. What so many of those people don't realize, though, is that the RHF pandemic was *good* for the country. It was cleansing. It allowed human behavior to take a more natural course. Humans thrive in the midst of adversity—at least, those who don't die."

He nodded toward Tessa, Latonya, Donica, and Sue. "Many of

us discovered that there are more important things than comfort and security. Our *cult*, as you call it, was actually a much more natural and satisfying way to exist. While others became stricken with fear or indecision about what to do, we came alive. It was magnificent, something we had never experienced before." He turned to his mates again. "Wouldn't you agree?"

All four women nodded. Donica said, "Infinity, you might not understand this, considering who you are, but never in your life can you feel so female—so deeply, inherently female—as when you have two men fight to the death to claim you as their mate."

"What in the living hell?" Emily whispered, barely loud enough for Infinity to hear.

Almost involuntarily, Infinity's hands turned to fists. "And so you intend to—"

"No!" Gibson said, holding up both hands. "You're misinterpreting. We have no intention of persuading this colony to adopt our beliefs and way of life. Let me finish. When the RHF pandemic subsided and order was restored, the country immediately started slipping back into its original pattern of complacency and moral decadence. Roaming bands of thieves, rapists, and murderers were captured or went back to their old lives. Packs of feral dogs were shot. Grocery stores and pharmacies removed the boards from their doors and windows and went back to business as usual. There were no more threats, no more hardships. What incentive did we have to continue our training? Guilds like ours, which were abundant and scattered everywhere, were condemned. All that had made us strong was being taken away."

Gibson gestured to the forest and rocky bluffs surrounding the group. "So we didn't sign up for this colony to change who you are. We signed up because we knew there would be hardships. We crave the challenges of survival. That's what makes us come alive."

"We couldn't even convince the other members of our guild to come with us," Donica added. "They were already sliding back to the old ways of life before RHF. They were ready to disband and go back to selling insurance, teaching school—whatever they'd been doing before."

"So now we're here, with you," Tessa said. "We'd like to be a part of this colony. But if you kick us out, we'll manage. Every hardship we face will only make us stronger. After all, it's the reason we're here in the first place."

Infinity sighed. Could these nutjobs be trusted? Their willingness to face danger would make them valuable to the colony. On the other hand, they were obviously frogshit crazy. And Gibson had even admitted to murdering at least one other man.

Desmond put his hand on Infinity's forearm. Almost immediately, silent words began flowing into her mind from his. "Here's a thought. Gibson has four mates. Those four make up a third of all female humans on this world. I don't suppose it has escaped his attention that he will be the one individual contributing the most DNA to all future humans on this world. Perhaps he wants to be the *Adam* of this version of Earth."

Infinity glanced at Desmond. She didn't have the ability to push her own thoughts back to his mind, but if it were possible she would have sent a mental image of her using a primitive spear to remove a specific appendage from Gibson's body.

"Well," said Steven, "it sounds like you wildcards are going to have one hell of a story for the rest of us. But as it stands now, I got no reason not to trust you. We got a little over an hour of daylight left. What do you say we grab them freshwater filters and head straight for the stream I found? We can be back here with several gallons of filtered water before dark." He grinned. "I promise I won't get lost this time."

Gibson nodded and started to get up. "Let's do it." He hesitated and turned to Infinity. "You okay with this plan?"

"We still need water," Infinity replied. "Give yourselves plenty of time to get back."

Emily jumped to her feet. "No way you're leaving without me this time, Steven."

Infinity and Desmond watched the team of seven head for the bunker to get the filters.

"You think those wildcards are going to be trouble?" Desmond asked.

She got to her feet and extended a hand to help him up. "Don't know yet. Probably."

They stepped around a pile of entrails and heads to join the other migrants who were watching Fisher, Hero, and Bard prepare the aquatic creatures for consumption. At least thirty pounds of meat, now cut into two-inch chunks, was arranged on a thin sheet of some kind of fabric or plastic. Fisher was crouched to the side, using a cutting tool to slice up several red fruits the size of a grapefruit. Hero and Bard stood over the meat, each of them squeezing slices of the fruit. Juice from the fruit dribbled onto the meat chunks, turning the meat from translucent pink to opaque white.

"The fruit seems to be highly acidic," Xavier offered. "I think they're chemically cooking the meat with the juice. They even showed me where to find these fruits. This lesson alone could be invaluable to our survival here."

Infinity watched as the beings stirred the meat with their fingers to turn the chunks over. Then they drizzled on more fruit juice. The meat was definitely cooking—without fire or heat. Of course, it was possible that the migrants' new friends had completely different nutritional needs, and that the meat of these sea creatures was toxic to humans. She assumed her group would eat the dehydrated meal packets until the supplies ran out, at which point they would know enough about the environment to gather their own food.

When the beings had squeezed every last drop from the fruits, Fisher took off again toward the beach. He returned after only a few minutes, carrying a bulging bag apparently made of the same material as the sheet under the meat. He climbed the rocky bluff, scuttled up to the cooking meat, and dumped the contents of the bag directly over it. At least thirty whale-salamander eggs spread out over the meat, the embryos inside still wriggling.

Bard spoke to the watching group. This time, Xavier's translator responded. "The eggs of the...*creature designation*...will give the food a good taste. We are fortunate to have these eggs, as they are abundant only for a limited time."

The outer jelly of the eggs quickly turned to liquid, and then the eggs themselves began bursting open, signaled by soft pops. First only a few eggs popped, and then more, sounding like a sputtering motorboat. The embryos stopped wriggling then faded from brown to light gray in color. Presumably, all of this was triggered by the acidic fruit juice.

Lenny crossed his arms. "Come on, you guys. Do I have to be the one to say it? Okay, I will. Lenny, in your infinite wisdom, you already knew that eating whale-salamander eggs was a good idea. You are an intellectual, as well as a physical, phenomenon."

Bard had been watching Lenny, but when none of the translators interpreted Lenny's words, the being spoke. Xavier's translator said, "This food is suitable for the needs of our bodies. We are hungry, and we will eat. We have prepared enough for you to eat, too. We would like to share it with you."

"We would be delighted to try it," said Hayley. "Thank you for teaching us how to prepare this food."

Infinity considered pointing out that the humans still had no idea how to catch the ocean creatures without getting themselves killed, but she decided not to dampen the mood.

Hayley passed out lightweight plates and sporks to everyone.

Fisher, Hero, and Bard accepted theirs, but then they set them aside and dug into the meal with their three-fingered hands. Crouching over the food, they skewered pieces of meat on their pointed fingertips and inserted them one at a time into the round holes in their faces. As they chewed, the squishy tissue around the holes twisted slightly in one direction and then the other, as if they were grinding the food in a circular motion instead of up and down.

Everyone else loaded their plates and started eating, which was followed by head nodding and murmurs of approval. Infinity spooned a few chunks onto her plate and took a nibble. The stuff was extremely fishy—no big surprise there—but she could get used to it. The meat was no worse than some of the giant bugs her colony had eaten for many months on the arthropod world.

Infinity looked around at the migrants' faces. She no longer saw signs of despair. Their eyes sparkled, and some of them were smiling and joking. She studied the strange beings who apparently wanted to become the migrants' friends. Their two-pronged tails seemed to loosen and tighten around their waists every few seconds as they ate, and the toes on their massive feet repeatedly flexed and curled, as if it felt good to dig the long digits into the dirt and leaves of the forest floor. The beings were completely alien in appearance. As Desmond had asked previously, how could these things possibly have evolved from any of the life forms of Earth? Especially on a world where the other creatures all seemed to be so... *normal.*

She shook her head and took another bite. Maybe none of that mattered. Her goal had been to live in peace with Desmond and her friends—her expanded family. Now that goal was becoming a reality.

As the group sat in a circle eating chemically-cooked salamander and fish, a raucous monkey-frog territory dispute arose in the distance.

INFINITY HAD WAITED on edge for Steven, Emily, and the wildcards to return. But the team not only had returned safely, they had brought seven bladders of filtered water, more than enough to quench everyone's thirst.

Infinity gathered the migrants together and insisted that the wildcards explain their history to the entire group. Gibson's mates mostly kept their mouths shut while he did the talking. Almost as if it were an afterthought, he added the detail about killing other men to claim Tessa, Sue, Donica, and Latonya as his mates. This resulted in murmurs of disbelief and a few angry protests, but then Gibson used his calm tone and smooth speaking style to make it seem as if this behavior had been commonplace and necessary during the RHF pandemic. Before long, the migrants were ready to turn their attention to other things.

Infinity now felt that she could at last sit down and try to relax. Dusk was bringing out waves of tiny insects, some of which were mosquito-like biters. The insects didn't bother Infinity much—she just threw on a long-sleeve shirt and long pants—but the others suddenly became motivated to decide on the sleeping arrangements.

Only nine tents had escaped destruction, which threatened to make things a bit awkward, but soon Gibson announced that all of the wildcards would occupy one tent. He and the four women didn't need much space to be comfortable, he explained. The others didn't seem surprised by this, having already heard Gibson's story. They finally decided on the wildcards in one tent, Lenny, Isabelle, and Daisy in another, Gideon and Armando would share one, and the couples in the six remaining tents: Desmond and Infinity, Xavier and Celia, Hayley and Alexander, Emily and Steven, Vic and Reyna, and the two doctors, Richard Hussain and Poppy Safran.

Before long, most of the exhausted migrants had retreated to their tents, leaving Infinity, Desmond, Lenny, and Xavier sitting on the ground around a small fire. Lenny had made the fire, and if his boasting could be believed, he had used only one match to do it.

Fisher, Hero, and Bard had disappeared into the forest to the east a few minutes ago, but now, in the last remaining daylight, they could be seen returning to the camp, walking at their full height. As the beings approached the fire, they bent their knees and returned to their normal squatting stance. Without exchanging words, Lenny and Xavier scooted around closer to Desmond and Infinity to make room, and the beings settled in across from the four humans.

This was the first time Infinity had seen them rest their rumps on the ground. With their knees still situated on either side of their heads, they unwound their tails from their waists, and the two tail tips pressed against each other below their chins, as if they were praying. Bard abruptly leaned to the side and touched the rubbery thing on his face—the protrusion Desmond had called a snood—to the same rubbery thing on Hero's face. The two snoods wrapped around each other for a moment, and then Bard pulled back and leaned in the other direction, repeating the same behavior with Fisher.

With almost synchronized motions, they used their small pairs of hands to lift the flaps covering the pouches at their waists. They each pulled out an object that appeared to be a tightly-wound length of cord.

They poked at the objects with their pointed fingers, teasing and loosening the cords. Using their two hands and two tail tips, they spread the cords, which turned out to be interconnected webs rather than single long strands. They began manipulating the string webs, pulling the strands one way and then the other with both hands and both tail tips, stretching the cords into complex patterns. They held each pattern in place for only a second or two before again manipulating the strands into a completely different pattern. As Infinity watched, mesmerized by the motions, the beings unfolded their shoulder limbs and inserted the prehensile tips into the mix, increasing the complexity of the movements by making a total of six points of contact with the strands.

Without slowing these movements, the three beings took their eyes off the dancing cords and gazed at Infinity and the other humans. Bard began speaking, pumping his arms slightly without interrupting the intricate movements. Infinity's translator said, "We find it interesting that the four of you are resting here while the others of your kind have taken shelter. Is there a significance to your bond with each other?"

Infinity had a hard time taking her eyes off the three gyrating webs of string. Apparently, the guys were just as transfixed because they weren't offering an answer. So, she forced herself to shift her gaze to Bard's face. "We have known each other longer than we've known most of the others. I guess you could say we're old friends. Do you mind if I ask what you're doing with those strings?"

"This is an activity that soothes us. It is something we do before we rest for the night."

Without pausing his shoulder-limbs, fingers, or tails, Fisher extended one of his long legs, wrapped his toes around a stick in the pile Lenny had collected, and gently inserted the stick into the fire. Then he extended the leg around the edge of the fire and pointed a ten-inch toe at Infinity's chest. He spoke, and her translator said, "You are different from your friends here. You look different and you speak differently. Are you a different species?"

Infinity realized Fisher was pointing to her breasts. "No, I'm the same species. I'm a female, and my friends here are males. There are twelve females in our group and ten males."

Fisher withdrew his foot. "Please explain."

Infinity glanced at Desmond. "A little help here?"

Desmond was still staring at the dancing strings, but he pulled his eyes away and returned her glance. "Okay, sure... but I don't know how well our translators will do with this." He turned to

Fisher. "Our species has two basic body structures—male and female. This is to facilitate sexual reproduction. Um, sexual reproduction involves combining genetic material from two individuals. This combining of genetic material is what allows animals to evolve over time, to gradually change, therefore adapting to changing environments. Most animals would go extinct without this ability."

He paused for a moment, apparently thinking, while his translator interpreted. After the translation ended, he put a hand to his chest and went on. "Therefore, we have males, like me. A male will pass genetic material to a female." He moved his hand to Infinity's shoulder. "The female takes that genetic material and combines it with her own. That combined genetic material then grows into a new individual, which has characteristics of both the female and the male."

"Wicked crisp tutorial, Des!" Lenny said while Desmond's translator clicked and buzzed. "You've done your species proud." Lenny then spoke to Fisher. "I'd like to point out how important it is that sexual reproduction results in variation of our offspring. Earlier you saw my baby girl Daisy? Daisy is my offspring. She's different from me and different from her mother. And Daisy's offspring will be different from her. This is how most animals evolve. It's abso-freaking-lutely essential to our existence."

"You're oversimplifying," Xavier said. "You haven't even mentioned the importance of genetic mutations." The translators recognized that he wasn't speaking to the beings and didn't interpret this.

"The nerd talk probably isn't necessary," Infinity interjected. "Fisher simply asked why I'm different. Besides, these guys may know more about this stuff than you do."

Lenny grinned. "Well, by cracky, let's find out." He turned to Fisher just as his translator finished interpreting his previous explanation. "We haven't been able to determine which of you are males and which are females. Can you help us understand how you reproduce?"

Fisher listened to the translation and then replied, "We understand what you have described, as we have studied many of the animals of this world, as well as many of the other types of living things. But we are not like the other animals of this world. We do not have males and females. Each of us is capable of producing offspring. Perhaps it would be a good way for you to get to know us if I were to explain. Would you like me to explain?"

Infinity could see the excitement in all three of the guys' faces. Personally, she didn't care much how these things made babies, as long as they didn't pose a threat to her colony, and at this moment she was truly beginning to believe the beings were going to be valuable allies.

"Yes, please explain," Desmond replied.

Before speaking again, Fisher leaned to the side and touched snoods with Bard, who then leaned to his side and did the same with Hero.

"What you have just seen is the way that we exchange genetic material." Fisher waited for the brief translation and then withdrew one of his hands from the string-stretching activity to point a finger at the snood on his face. "Genetic material is present within the fluid on the underside of this...*body part designation*." He returned his hand to its ongoing job of creating complex string patterns. "We exchange genetic material often, particularly when we are near other individuals we respect. I'm sure you must understand why we do not exchange genetic material with those we do not respect."

Again, he disengaged his hand and placed the center finger on a bulge of flesh beside his snood. "The genetic material we have received is stored here. We can hold this genetic material here for a long time. We can hold it all our lives if we wish to. When we are ready to produce an offspring, our bodies will know this and will make use of some of the genetic material we have been storing here."

Fisher stuck the tip of his finger under the edge of the fleshy bulge and lifted, revealing a dark cavity about an inch long, a feature Infinity hadn't noticed before. Fisher said, "An offspring will begin to grow within this pouch. When the offspring becomes too large for the pouch, we pull it out of the pouch and give it to our caretakers. Some of us are particularly suited to feeding and nurturing our offspring, and those individuals become our caretakers. As the offspring grows larger, our caretakers teach it how to feed itself and how to speak. Eventually they teach it how to perform tasks that are useful to our city."

Fisher waited for the translation to catch up before saying, "I have now explained how each of us is capable of producing offspring. As with your species, and as with most of the other animal species on this world, we produce offspring that are different from us, allowing us to evolve. But you, and most of the other animals on this world, combine genetic material from two individuals, whereas our offspring result from combining genetic material from multiple individuals."

After the translation finished, Desmond, Lenny, and Xavier remained silent, staring, apparently speechless.

Infinity nudged Desmond. "While you guys are having brain orgasms, I'm going to ask the obvious question we should have asked in the first place." She turned to the three beings. "Why is it, exactly, that you are so different from us and from all the other animals on this world?"

After her translator stopped clicking and buzzing, the beings gazed at her silently. Seconds passed. The extended silence made it seem as if all four eyes of each individual were studying her, seeing her for the first time. Bard actually stopped manipulating his string.

Infinity shifted her position slightly and glanced at Desmond, frowning.

Finally, Bard spoke and Infinity's translator said, "As we have said, the black-fur beings created us."

Infinity waited for more, but Bard didn't go on. "Why?" she asked.

"We do not know why."

Infinity sighed. None of this really even mattered anyway. Besides, she was exhausted. She nudged Desmond again. "You ready to turn in?"

He blinked at her, as if he hadn't even considered it yet. "Okay. Sure."

They both started to get up, but then Bard spoke again. "We are pleased that the black-fur beings have sent you to this world. We do not know why they sent you here, but we are pleased."

Hero added, "Perhaps you were sent here because we have failed. Perhaps the black-fur beings do not like our city."

Fisher said, "The black-fur beings provided us with a production factory to create the components of our city. Perhaps we have not used our production factory properly."

Bard continued this twisted line of reasoning. "You beings were sent here to teach us how to properly use our production factory. We are pleased that you will teach us."

Fisher said, "But you will then want us to destroy our city so that we can produce a better city. This will take a long time, and the progress we've made will be lost."

Infinity finished getting to her feet, and she held up both her hands. "Wait! We didn't come here to teach you anything, or to make you destroy your city. Do you guys realize you kind of have a problem with jumping to conclusions? You're getting all worked up over nothing."

The beings listened to the translation, and again they stared at her in silence. After at least thirty seconds, Bard spoke. "The black-fur beings have sent you here to teach us how to not jump to conclusions."

Hero said, "Yes, you will teach us to not get all worked up over nothing."

Then Fisher added, "We will learn what you teach us, and then we will use what we have learned as we continue to improve our city."

Infinity turned to Desmond. "I need some goddamn sleep."

10

———

STORIES

MAY 3 - 5:41 AM

DESMOND HAD no idea what time it was, but the forest outside the tent was pitch black. He had to pee for the first time since bridging to this world the previous morning. He sat up and pulled on his t-shirt and shoes.

Infinity stirred. "Where you going?"

"Just need to move around. Can't sleep anyway. I won't go far."

She put a hand on his shoulder and pulled him down toward her. As he hugged her, she bit down gently on his earlobe and whispered, "If moving around is what you need, I have a better idea."

He kissed her neck and then pulled back. "That's extraordinarily tempting, but I actually need to do a little more than move around."

She snorted a brief laugh. "I was only half serious anyway. Still tired as hell."

He kissed her lips. "I'll see you when you wake up then." The tent zipper was loud, so he opened the door just enough to crawl through. After zipping it shut, he got to his feet and saw hints of orange light peeking through the trees to the east. The sun would be rising soon. He breathed in the damp morning air. No telling what the new day might bring.

He made his way over to the jumbled boulders on the uphill side of the camp, relieved himself, then turned and scanned the surrounding area. A dark figure was standing at the drop-off on the other side of camp, so he moved silently between the tents to see who it was. As he drew near, he could make out the columns and rows of symbols tattooed on Celia Pickett's bare back. She was standing there alone, looking out toward the beach.

"Morning, Celia," Desmond said softly to avoid startling her before stepping up to her side.

She glanced at him. "Hi, Des." She went back to gazing north.

Desmond wasn't surprised she was topless. During the months his colony had lived on the arthropod world, she had made a habit of wearing only shoes and shorts made from the belly skin of giant isopods. She wanted the tattoos on her back to serve as a reminder to give hope to her fellow colonists that they'd be rescued. The tattoos were actually symbols—nine hundred, making up the key to unlocking the true power of bridging technology. Eventually, though, the colonists had grown to love their existence on the arthropod world, and their previous hopes for rescue became irrelevant. Celia, however, continued to prefer minimal clothing.

Desmond followed her gaze to the north. The forest blocked the view of the beach, but orange flickers of reflected sunlight from the water made their way through the foliage like flashing fireflies. "I bet I know what you're thinking," Desmond said. "You're missing our old life on the arthropod world. I miss it too."

She nodded in the semidarkness. "Yeah. It was a good life, wasn't it? I suppose now I should just be happy to be alive, and for my baby to be alive too." She put her hand on her swollen belly.

Desmond glanced down at her bulge. She still had two months

to go, but Celia was petite, which exaggerated her belly's size. "Have you and Xavier thought of a name?"

"We're thinking Alpha. Boy or girl, doesn't matter."

"The first human born on this world?"

She nodded and rubbed her hand over her belly. "The little squirt needs something to be proud of, don't you think?"

"Yeah, it's perfect."

"Maybe you and Infinity will be next."

Desmond eyed her. The members of his expanded family had long ago made a point of not mentioning such things to Infinity or him. But now that Kitty had performed some kind of surgical procedure on Infinity to repair the damage suffered long ago from a knife fight, the topic was apparently fair game.

"I guess time will tell," he said. He almost stated it would be wise to wait until they determined how safe this world would be, but he stopped himself. Celia definitely didn't need to hear that. Instead, he decided to steer the talk in a different direction. "You know what I want to see?"

"What's that?"

"I want to see how you're going to explain to Alpha why you have nine hundred symbols on your back, and the whole sequence of events leading up to that. I don't envy you that task."

She chuckled. "Or how I'll explain why Armando has the exact same symbols on his back."

"I bet Armando will teach Alpha to call him Grandpa Doyle. He's told us more than once that he wants *grandkids* from us." Desmond made quotes in the air when he said the word grandkids.

She chuckled again. "Yeah, I've heard the same spiel."

Celia once was Armando's highly valued assistant, back when Armando had been the director of SafeTrek Bridging. Under his stuffy, professional veneer was a fatherly and caring man, and Desmond imagined he was as close to Celia as he was to Infinity.

A movement at the west end of camp caught Desmond's eye.

He turned and squinted. The area was still pretty dark, but he saw several figures bending this way and that. It was Fisher, Hero, and Bard, and it looked like they were actually stretching.

Desmond nudged Celia's shoulder. "Let's go say good morning to our new friends, shall we?" They both headed that way.

As they drew nearer, Desmond realized the stretching routine was more complex than he thought. Each being was standing on one foot, with all seven other appendages simultaneously extending outward and then folding back up. At the same time, each being was bending and then extending his supporting leg, lowering his whole body nearly to the ground and then lifting it back to its full height.

The beings turned their heads to gaze at Desmond and Celia, but they didn't speak, so Desmond remained quiet to avoid rudely interrupting what most likely was a silent ritual. The three beings switched to standing on the other leg and continued their exercises for several more minutes as the orange glow in the eastern sky intensified.

"Maybe we should leave them alone," Celia whispered.

Seconds later, Bard retracted his limbs and settled into his normal crab-like stance. This apparently prompted Hero and Fisher to do the same.

Bard spoke and Celia's translator responded. "As the light of a new day begins to illuminate us, we like to awaken our bodies and contemplate the mystery of our presence on this world. We will now go to the water to continue our contemplations. You should come with us to the water. We would enjoy speaking to you."

Desmond scanned the camp. All the others were still sleeping, apparently. He turned to Celia. "Are you up for a walk? I doubt there will be any danger as long as we're with these guys."

She rubbed her belly. "I think walking would be good for us." She turned to Bard. "We would like that, thank you."

Bard and Hero took a moment to lean toward each other and

entwine their snoods. The three beings retrieved their waist packs from their shelter. Hero lifted one of his long legs, pointed a toe at Celia's swollen abdomen, and said, "We will walk slowly with you, if you wish."

Desmond realized this comment must have involved significant deduction, considering Hero's species experienced nothing remotely similar to human pregnancy. Even if Hero had studied reproductive biology of the local animals, he would probably be unfamiliar with mammalian placental pregnancy, a single large fetus developing within the female's body.

Instead of leaping directly over the drop-off, the beings walked beside Desmond and Celia to the west and skirted the rocky bluff. As they approached the swamp separating the beach from the hillside, Bard spoke and Celia's translator interpreted. "You have told us that you come from a world that no longer exists. We would like for you to tell us more about that world. Why does it no longer exist?"

Desmond considered this. If he told the truth, would these beings worry that the same thing would now happen to their world?

Celia said, "That world was actually a different version of this one, in an alternate timeline—an alternate universe. Unfortunately, that world collapsed upon itself, and billions of people died."

As Celia's translator interpreted, the group came upon the swamp's edge. In the faint pre-dawn light, the water was black and foreboding, but Bard and his companions simply extended their legs to lift their bodies higher and began wading.

Desmond held out a hand to Celia.

"I've walked through this a half dozen times," she said. "I'll be fine."

They entered the knee-deep swamp. Desmond felt slimy whale-salamander eggs oozing against his legs as they sloshed their way to the other side.

Emerging from the swampy forest onto the beach, Desmond

stopped to stare at the sparkling orange reflections on the water's surface. The leading edge of the sun was just starting to peek over the horizon, making for a spectacular scene, although the offshore islands were still dark, mysterious masses in the distance. The ocean breeze smelled fresh, and he inhaled the pleasant scent of plankton, algae, and wet sand.

Bard, Hero, and Fisher had settled back to their squatting stance and were waiting for them about fifty yards out on the beach. As Desmond and Celia approached, Fisher said, "Why did your world collapse upon itself?"

Desmond's eyes met Celia's. "I don't know how much we should tell them," he said, knowing his translator wouldn't interpret this.

She shrugged slightly. "If we expect to be long-time friends, why not be honest about everything?"

Desmond turned to Fisher. "Our story is not a happy one. In fact, it's tragic and horrifying. Our world collapsed because of something we did. Our scientists discovered a signal that was being transmitted through space from another civilization. The signal contained information. A *lot* of information. Including instructions for constructing a specific type of device. The device allowed us to travel—to bridge—from our world to alternate versions of our world."

Desmond paused to allow the translation to catch up. As the three beings listened, they began moving. Fisher stepped to the left while Hero and Bard stepped to the right. They slowly scuttled around Desmond and Celia until they were between the humans and the swamp.

As Desmond and Celia turned so that they could still face the beings, Bard spoke. "We would like for you to tell us more."

Desmond again looked at Celia, who was now frowning. He was getting used to strange behavior in these beings, but he found their sudden shift in position unnerving. He continued. "We constructed a bridging device. Actually, our species constructed seven of the devices. We began using them. We bridged people to alternate versions of our world, mainly to conduct research about how living things, as well as the planet itself, would evolve in different timelines. It was fascinating, and we learned a lot from it." He hesitated, thinking about what to say next. "But it was a mistake. We didn't know it at the time, but the bridging devices were all producing billions of very small and very heavy particles. These particles sank to the center of our planet. They gradually accumulated there until it was too late. This destroyed our world, causing it to implode upon itself."

The rising sun was casting more light with every passing second, illuminating the beings' faces and bodies, and it seemed as if their skin was now rapidly shifting from green to brown. Desmond had no way of understanding their facial expressions, of course, but their body language was enough to ratchet up his alarm. All three beings spread their legs slightly and hoisted their bodies higher, behaviors Desmond assumed were universal indicators of readiness for action.

"Is everything okay?" Desmond asked. "Are you upset about something?"

After the translation, Bard repeated, "We would like for you to tell us more."

Desmond studied the three beings for a moment. They simply stared back at him. "Okay, well, it turns out the civilization—we called them the Outlanders—that sent out the instructions for bridging technology had done this on purpose. They had intentionally sent instructions for a device that destroys entire worlds. It was their way of eliminating other civilizations, an unthinkably ruthless act. Eight billion of our species were killed, as well as every other living thing on our world. Only a few of us escaped by bridging to alternate versions of our world. We are among those few." Desmond decided to stop there.

The beings remained stone-still as they listened to the translation. Desmond's heart was now pounding, although he wasn't sure exactly why.

The beings spoke to each other. Finally, Fisher turned and addressed Desmond and Celia. Desmond's translator said, "We are glad that you have told us more information. Now we will tell you more information. We would like for you to listen."

After the translation, Desmond said, "Okay, we'll listen."

Bard took over, pumping his arms and generating a long sequence of buzzes and clicks. Finally, he paused, and Desmond's translator responded. "You have told us that the black-fur beings sent you here. We have told you that we know of the black-fur beings. We have not seen the black-fur beings in many generations, but we know of them. The black-fur beings taught our ancestors how to live on this world. The black-fur beings provided us with a production factory so that we can make the materials we need. The black-fur beings also told us a story. This story is important to us. I will now tell this story to you, and you will listen."

Yet again, Desmond exchanged frowns with Celia.

Bard continued then waited while Desmond's translator interpreted. "The black-fur beings knew of the civilization that created the instructions for bridging technology. You have said that you call this civilization the... Outlanders. The black-fur beings received these instructions, just as you did. You followed the instructions and destroyed your world. The black-fur beings did not follow the instructions. Instead, they studied the instructions. Very carefully they studied the instructions. Do you know what they found within the instructions?"

Desmond's internal alarm went into overdrive. Kitty's people—the black-fur beings—had made it abundantly clear that sharing the key to bridging technology with another civilization was a violation of their rules. In fact, the consequence of this violation was either total annihilation or a forced, brutal trial, which gave the violator only a slim chance of avoiding annihilation. Suddenly, he was acutely aware that the key was standing just beside him, tattooed onto Celia's back. He and Celia needed to proceed with caution.

"We know the instructions contain hidden information that can be used to unlock certain functions of the bridging device," he said. Confirming knowledge of the key was not the same thing as sharing the key's actual content.

Bard said, "Yes, the black-fur beings told us that. The black-fur beings also told us they had found more information hidden deeper within the instructions. This information required additional effort to discover and interpret."

"Yes, they told us this also. There are multiple layers of information, and each layer is more difficult to access than the last. We were told that these layers were keys, and each key could unlock more capabilities of bridging technology."

"Did your species discover the keys?" Bard asked.

Desmond turned to Celia and pressed a finger to his lips, requesting that she allow him to provide answers. He figured the gesture would be meaningless to Bard. He tried to provide a noncommittal response to Bard's question. "We became aware of the first-layer key. Later we figured out the second-layer key."

Bard was silent for a moment after listening to the translation. Then he spoke again. "The black-fur beings discovered many layers. Some of the deepest layers are not keys to bridging technology. They contain other information."

Was Bard offering to provide this information? If so, Desmond had to refuse. If humans accepted the information without being capable of discovering it on their own, this would definitely be a violation. Perhaps this was another test Kitty's people had devised, to see if humans would make the same mistake a second time.

"That is interesting and surprising," Desmond said.

Bard spoke and then paused to wait for the translation. "Yes. In fact, the deepest layer that the black-fur beings discovered was the most interesting and surprising of all the layers."

Desmond was tempted to ask what it contained, but he remained silent, waiting.

Bard continued. "The beings you call the Outlanders desired, above all else, to influence other civilizations. They developed an impressive and formidable civilization of their own, but they were not content with this. They wished to impose their ideologies upon other civilizations. In fact, as you know, they even devised and implemented a plan to destroy other civilizations, based upon their own criteria for judging which civilizations were worthy and which were not."

After this translation, Hero spoke. "You and the surviving members of your species must certainly consider the Outlanders' plan to be unjust and unmerited. Do you agree?"

Desmond didn't hesitate. "Of course we agree."

Bard said, "And we agree as well. The plan was unjust and unmerited."

After this brief translation, the three beings stood there silently, still maintaining stances that indicated readiness to act.

Although their words were not threatening, Desmond was pretty sure they did not intend to allow him and Celia to return to camp. He was now glad the beings hadn't brought their rifles to the beach. "Is something wrong?" he asked. "Have we offended you in some way?"

Bard replied. "You have not offended us. But we would like for you to listen to us."

"We *are* listening."

Bard continued. "The black-fur beings do not agree with you. The black-fur beings told us they believe the Outlanders' plan to be just and merited."

Desmond nodded then realized nodding probably meant nothing to these beings. "Yes, they made that extremely clear to us."

"The black-fur beings told us that they revere the Outlanders. The black-fur beings admire the Outlanders to an extraordinary degree."

Desmond nodded again. "Yes, we know that to be true."

"So the black-fur beings were particularly interested in the deepest layer of information within the Outlanders' transmitted signal."

Again, Desmond waited, trying to avoid flat-out asking about the content of the information layer.

After at least half a minute, Bard spoke again. "The Outlanders placed within this layer an extensive set of information about their own genetic material. The layer contained enough information for the black-fur beings to create a population of beings—a population of new Outlanders."

As the translation ended, Desmond's stomach began to knot—even before he fully comprehended what Bard had said. In the seconds of silence that followed, the knot grew tighter, making it difficult to breathe.

Bard spoke again. "The Outlanders wished to travel to other worlds in their own universe. They had already learned that traveling to distant worlds is simply not possible. So, they transmitted information about their own genetic material. They buried the information in such a way that it could only be discovered and understood by highly intelligent beings. The black-fur beings are highly intelligent."

It was all coming together now. Desmond forced himself to take a deep breath, but the air caused a hitch in his chest. He coughed, then wiped his mouth with the back of his hand. He took another deep breath and focused on Bard's face. The sun was mostly above the horizon now, and its reflection could be seen in all four of the being's eyes.

"Desmond, what's going on? What is he telling us?"

Desmond ignored Celia and spoke to Bard. "You said that the

black-fur beings created you and put you on this world. Your species... you're the new Outlanders, aren't you?"

The three beings listened to the translation, then shifted their stances slightly, becoming even more primed for action.

"Oh my God," Celia whispered.

Fisher spoke. "Did you come here for retribution?"

Desmond swallowed. He and the other migrants had not come here for retribution. No, they hadn't. No. He swallowed again. But the Outlanders had killed eight billion people. Almost everyone Desmond had ever known. His mother. They had destroyed every creature and natural ecosystem he had loved and had hoped to devote his life to studying. He wiped his mouth again and stared at Bard, then at Hero, and at Fisher. The beings hadn't changed in the last two minutes, but now they looked different to Desmond—more menacing.

Desmond turned to Celia. She was gone. He snapped around and spotted her, now twenty yards away, staring out toward the surf and the sea. He spun back around to face the beings.

"Did you come here for retribution?" Fisher asked again.

Desmond wasn't so sure now. Something deep within him was starting to boil up. Eight billion people. His mom. All killed, and for what? He squeezed his hands into fists. The boiling within him was raw hatred. It was a drive, an urge, perhaps even an instinct, overwhelming him and ordering him to lunge at these bastards and beat them until they were dead. Right here on the beach.

The three beings looked at each other and slowly unfurled their forked tails from around their waists.

But these beings hadn't actually destroyed his world, had they? It was their genetic ancestors, all of whom had probably died thousands of years ago. Apparently Fisher, Hero, and Bard were of the same species, perhaps even exact clones of specific Outlanders who had come up with the world-destroying plan. Desmond shook his head, trying to clear his thoughts. He opened and closed his fists, forcing his hands to relax. He had almost done it. He had almost attacked these beings who had been mostly friendly so far.

Instead of answering Bard's question, Desmond said, "Do you intend to kill us, like you killed the beings at that other camp?"

Bard said, "We do not want to be killed. We will do what is necessary to prevent your retribution."

Desmond took deep, even breaths, and the knot in his stomach loosened slightly. He could handle this. He could get his burning hatred under control. He just needed time to think. Finally, he said, "We did not come here for retribution."

The three beings shifted their gazes and stared at something over Desmond's shoulder. Abruptly they rose to their full height.

Something shot by Desmond's elbow from behind. "Murderers! I'll fucking kill you!" Celia cried, swinging a four-foot piece of driftwood. She hit one of Bard's long legs, crumpling the being onto his side. She raised the wood again and slammed it down onto Bard's outstretched hands.

For a few long seconds Desmond was frozen in place, shocked at first, then unsure whether he wanted to stop Celia or help her pulverize these Outlanders. That, of course, would be suicide for the entire human colony. He stepped forward. "Celia, stop!"

As Desmond reached to grab her arms and restrain her, Hero thrust out one of his long legs and kicked Celia, throwing her back into Desmond. Celia's head struck Desmond's chin, and the momentum of her body knocked both of them to the ground.

Celia immediately began moaning and gasping for air, the wind knocked completely out of her.

Desmond rolled from beneath her. "Celia! Are you okay?"

She writhed on the sand, holding her swollen abdomen with both hands. She could barely suck in any air, but she managed to gasp, "My... baby!"

He rolled her slightly toward her back. A large footprint, with sand ground into the skin, was visible on her chest and one breast—several inches above her baby bulge. She continued gasping for air.

Desmond jumped up and faced off with the Outlanders. Bard spoke as he was getting to his feet, and Desmond's translator said, "You have come for retribution."

"No, we haven't come for retribution!" Desmond shouted. "We still want to be your friends. But adjusting to this news isn't going to be easy for us." He pointed down at Celia. "Surely you can see that."

"Hey, Desmond! What's going on?" It was Gideon's voice.

Desmond looked past the Outlanders. Gideon and Steven were wading through the swamp, about to emerge onto the beach.

Desmond turned back to the three beings. "We need some time. I can talk to my people. I can explain everything. I'll convince them not to seek retribution. But you need to go. Please trust me. You need to go *now*. Maybe come back in a few days. Do you understand?"

The Outlanders listened to the translation while Celia continued gasping.

"They're in trouble!" Desmond heard Gideon say to Steven. The two men sloshed their way out of the swamp and began running across the beach.

"You need to go now!" Desmond pleaded.

Hero, still at his full height, took a step forward, looking down at Celia. Then he turned to Desmond and spoke.

Before Desmond's translator even began interpreting Hero's words, the three Outlanders lumbered past him directly toward the surf.

Desmond's translator then said, "We understand. We will go to our city now. Do not go to our city. When we return, we will be prepared. We do not want to kill you, but we will if we must."

"What the hell happened here?" Gideon demanded as he came

to a stop. He and Steven kneeled next to Celia, who was just now starting to catch her breath.

Desmond watched the Outlanders as they splashed through the surf. When they were up to their knees, they dove gracefully into the sea and disappeared.

11

GENETICS

MAY 3 - 6:52 AM

INFINITY OPENED HER EYES. She thought she'd heard a distant voice. There it was again. It sounded like someone was calling for Richard. She sat up. Richard Hussain was the group's obstetrician.

"Richard! We need you down here!" It was Desmond's voice.

Infinity pulled on her t-shirt and shoes, zipped open the door, and crawled out of the tent. Several other migrants were emerging from their tents as well, including Richard and his partner, Poppy.

Richard turned, looking around at the surrounding hillside and forest. "Who's calling my name?"

Xavier emerged from his tent. "Where's Celia? I woke up and she wasn't here."

"Richard! We need you. Down by the swamp!"

"That's Desmond," Infinity said.

Richard ducked into his tent and grabbed his medical back-pack. "Let's go!"

Infinity started jogging to the west, followed by Richard, Poppy,

Xavier, and the others. They skirted the end of the bluff and headed down toward the swamp. Why would Desmond call out specifically for Richard? Poppy had been a SafeTrek med tech and was more skilled at emergency medical care. There had to be a problem with Celia. What the hell was Celia doing down by the beach at this hour?

"Over here!" Desmond shouted as the group approached the swamp.

Infinity corrected her course and spotted Desmond standing over Gideon and Steven, who were on their knees with Celia sitting between them, apparently hunched over in pain.

As Infinity came to a stop, Desmond said, "We carried her through the swamp, but we didn't want to go any farther without Richard's approval."

Xavier ran up beside Infinity, dropped to his knees, and grabbed Celia's hand. "Shit, what happened?"

Richard arrived and kneeled before Celia. "What's wrong, hon? Where do you hurt?"

Celia put her free hand on her chest, but she was sobbing and struggling to catch her breath. Richard pulled her hand away, revealing a red impact wound. Droplets of blood were oozing from numerous pinholes, apparently where grains of sand had been driven into the skin.

"My... baby!" Celia cried between labored breaths.

Richard prodded her belly from several sides, then he zipped open his pack and pulled out a stethoscope. "Try to relax, Celia. Breathe normally if you can, okay?" He put the stethoscope in his ears and listened to her abdomen. Celia continued sobbing, but everyone else fell silent. Richard moved the scope to a different position. After several seconds he moved it again and then again to another spot. He held it there for a good thirty seconds.

Xavier placed his forehead against Celia's and started whispering soothing words to her. Her sobs diminished a bit.

Finally, Richard took the stethoscope and transferred it from his ears to Celia's. "Listen, hon. Calm down and listen carefully. Do you hear that?"

Celia closed her eyes, appearing to try her best to control her breathing. She opened her eyes. "It's... my baby. It's Alpha."

Richard pulled the device from her ears. "That's right. At the moment, your baby is fine. We'll get you back to camp, and I'll examine you more carefully, okay?"

She nodded. "Okay." Then she looked up at Desmond. "Tell them, Des."

Infinity turned to Desmond. The look on his face was one Infinity had rarely seen—lips pursed into a frown, eyes unwilling to meet her gaze. There was something he definitely did *not* want to say.

"One of the beings hurt her," Gideon offered. "Hero, I think. Steven and I were just getting to the beach." He then turned to Desmond, brows raised, waiting for an explanation.

"You... have to... tell them!" Celia said.

Desmond's frown deepened, and he shook his head slightly. "Yes, I do need to tell you all something, but I'm extremely concerned about your possible reaction. I... well, my own reaction was surprising, even to me. I could hardly get it under control. Celia *wasn't* able to control herself. She attacked Bard, and Hero was simply blocking her attack. I think he intentionally avoided harming her baby."

Infinity felt adrenaline building in her bloodstream. Desmond had hesitated to explain things before, but this was different. Something was seriously wrong. "Maybe you should just tell us what the hell's going on."

He nodded once. "Yeah. I just... I'm scared, Infinity."

Her adrenaline surged. Desmond rarely said he was scared, even when he was. She looked down at Celia. "Maybe you should tell us."

Desmond grabbed Infinity's elbow. "No! I'll tell you. First, though, I want to remind you that our survival here depends on us getting along with Hero and the rest of his species. We have to coexist with them. That's why Kitty's people sent us here in the first place, remember?"

Infinity stared at him. "Okay, you've reminded us. Now, why did Hero hurt Celia?"

Desmond sighed. "Please think carefully about everything I say before you react. You know how we thought Kitty's people seemed to almost worship the Outlanders? Well, we were right. They found a layer of information in the Outlanders' radio signal that contained details about the Outlanders themselves."

Desmond was talking faster now. "That information included the actual genetic code for the Outlander species. Maybe it was a general sequence for the species, maybe it was exact codes for specific individuals—I don't know. Kitty's people took that information and actually created Outlanders. In fact, they created several entire populations. For what reason, I have no idea. They put those populations on several worlds, provided them with some kind of factory for producing raw materials, and then taught them what they needed to know for survival. We are now on a world with one of those populations. I told Hero, Bard, and Fisher to go home for now. I wanted to talk to you guys, to make sure we don't overreact and do something we will regret."

He paused, apparently out of breath.

Gideon made a soft huffing sound. "You're saying Hero, Bard, and Fisher are *Outlanders*?"

Desmond nodded. "Yes, but not really. They're the same species, I suppose. But these beings are—"

Infinity turned her back on Desmond and stopped listening. She didn't want to hear any more. She had to think. She took several steps away from the group, rubbing her forehead with one hand. The Outlanders? Here? Graphic scenes began flashing through her mind—scenes she had tried for many months to forget. Hundreds of refugees lying injured and dead outside SafeTrek, having had nowhere to hide when a freak storm hit. Terrified refugees storming into SafeTrek's lobby, only to be gunned down by soldiers who were just as scared. The carcass of a dog—someone's companion—waterlogged and stinking by the side of the road after the Mississipi river had actually flowed north during an earthquake, flooding entire cities. Desmond, looking his mother in the eyes and saying goodbye because he failed to secure a position for her in an outgoing colony. Infinity then saw her younger self, standing on the street in front of her parents' old house, wondering if they still lived there, knowing she'd never see them again but refusing to walk up and knock on the door.

She raised her other hand and began rubbing her head with both palms. Something inside her abruptly snapped. She actually heard it, like a switch being flipped or a twig breaking. The visions of the past stopped appearing, maybe because she just couldn't take any more. Or maybe because she needed to focus on other things. She realized what was overwhelming her. It was her own guilt. She had caused all that pain and death. She was a bridger, and bridgers were responsible for what had happened. She was responsible, and she was goddamn tired of suffering the guilt.

The truth was, someone else was even more responsible—the Outlanders. The Outlanders were the real cause of Earth's destruction. Therefore, they were the real cause of her endless, soul-sucking guilt.

Infinity lowered her hands and opened her eyes. She turned back to the others, who were still questioning Desmond. What else could they possibly need to know? Her chest was heaving, and she felt like she couldn't get enough oxygen, but now she didn't care about that. "We have three of their rifles," she said loudly.

Desmond and the others stopped talking and turned to her. Several of them nodded, as if they knew what she was thinking.

She stepped closer. "We also have spears, knives, and hatchets. I don't know how many Outlanders there are. They told us they have a city, but maybe our translators chose that word. Maybe what they actually have is a small settlement. We need to find it and assess how vulnerable they are. Maybe we pick them off one at a time whenever they move away from the main population. Or maybe we can enter at night when they're sleeping. We can move through their dwellings silently—take them out with the knives and hatchets."

"We need to see their city," Gideon said. "I'm guessing it's to the west, since that's the direction those sons-of-bitches came from. It's probably not far. They rode their frog-steeds here instead of using their submarine or whatever other vehicles they have. Not only that, but it makes sense that Kitty would bridge us to a spot near the Outlanders' city."

Desmond said, "You guys can't be serious! Why are you even talking about this? We were sent here to get along with them!"

Infinity stared at him. She felt confused, unsure why he would question what obviously needed to be done. She stepped closer. "Desmond, what's wrong?"

"What's wrong?" he almost shouted. "You're talking about committing suicide, that's what's wrong! Do you not remember the consequences for defying Kitty's rules?"

Hayley spoke up. "What Desmond is saying makes sense. I'm as outraged as anyone that Kitty's people would send us here to cozy up with the very beings who destroyed our world. But what's done is done—we need to look to the future. Don't you all agree?"

Richard stood from where he'd been kneeling beside Celia and pointed a finger at Hayley. "Whose future are you referring to? Ours? Because I don't see much of a future in becoming friends with the Outlanders. How could we ever look at those bastards again without thinking about what they've done?"

"That's right," Xavier said. "How am I supposed to forgive

them for what Hero did to Celia, let alone to every member of my family back home? Celia could have miscarried. She *still* might."

"I'm in agreement with Xavier and Richard," said Lenny. "You want to talk about the future, Hayley? Maybe our future here isn't what we should be worried about. Think about what Kitty and her people are trying to do. They're trying to seed an entire new Outlander civilization, and Kitty has made it clear that we are here to help the Outlanders develop to their full potential. Their full freaking potential! We all know what that means. Well, I don't *want* to help them do it. I don't *want* to help this new Outlander civilization become as ruthless and destructive as the originals. They'll have the same desire to destroy other civilizations. *Entire* civilizations. You don't actually want to help with that, do you?"

Desmond was shaking his head, obviously refusing to see the logic in all this. "I don't think that's what these beings intend to do. Bard made it clear that they believe the actions of their genetic ancestors were unjust and unmerited." He made a point of looking directly at Infinity. "What about our future together? What about the fact that we're sick and tired of violence and destruction? We have a chance to live here in peace."

Infinity took two more steps closer to Desmond. He was the only person she had ever really loved—she had to make him understand. This was a chance for absolution for them both, and he should see that. After all, he was almost as guilty as she was. He had been a bridger too. She said, "I want that future as much as you do. But I know you agree with me. Deep down inside, you have to know that we could never live side-by-side with the Outlanders. How could we possibly hold on to any dignity we have left? This is just another of Kitty's cruel games. Once again, she has thrown us into a nightmare with impossible choices. Please tell me you're with me on this."

He stared at her as if he didn't even recognize her. She could see he didn't agree, even though the logic was as plain as day, and even though he could see how important it was to her. Infinity felt a hollowness forming inside her, a sensation she hadn't felt since before she met Desmond. In the last two years he had somehow filled that hollowness—had made her feel less alone. Now he was taking all that away.

She realized the other migrants were talking, some of them arguing, even yelling. She didn't care. She needed to make Desmond understand. She took one more step and grabbed his arm, perhaps gripping it tighter than necessary.

"Maybe we can't kill them all," she said to him. "But dammit, we can kill some of them. We can show Kitty's people that we're not willing to be part of their insane plan."

Desmond wasn't even listening to her now. He was glancing to the side, looking at the other migrants. Ignoring her. The hollowness became almost overwhelming, so she balled her fists and transformed the pain into something more useful—anger.

"Hey, listen up!"

Infinity snapped her head to the side. It took her a moment to realize Gibson was the one who had shouted.

"Listen to me a minute," he said.

The migrants finally fell silent.

Gibson continued. "I know right now some of you are keen on revenge. I get that. But before you go off and get us all killed, you need to at least understand what's happening here."

Gideon pointed a finger at Gibson. "Your opinion means exactly squat. You're not really even part of this group, wildcard. So, keep your—"

"Just hear me out!" Gibson shouted.

Infinity turned away from Desmond and considered punching the damn wildcard.

Gibson went on. "There's a fancy name for it, 5-HTT-something, but the popular name is the *revenge gene*. Some of us have it, some of us don't. How do I know this? Because of all the nastiness that resulted from the RHF pandemic on our world. People did terrible things to other people. Rape, murder, torture—you name it. The thing is, the violence didn't end when the pandemic was under control. That's when revenge started. People who had done unthinkable things tried to go back to their jobs, their homes, and their families, but many of them had left surviving victims in their wake. Some of those survivors wanted revenge. For years those people went to great lengths to locate the ones who had hurt them or their loved ones. It was such a common phenomenon that it became a subject of scientific study."

Infinity was getting tired of this. "You going to make a point or not?"

Gibson nodded. "Bear with me." He glanced around the group. "How many of you agree with Infinity, that we should find the Outlanders' settlement and attack them? There's a reason I'm asking, so please just raise your hand."

Infinity lifted her hand. As did Gideon, and then Lenny. Within a few seconds, Xavier, Celia, Richard, Poppy, Emily, and Steven had also raised their hands. Finally, Armando slowly lifted his hand. Good—maybe Armando would be able to get through to Desmond.

"Okay," Gibson said. "How many of you—even though you're outraged at what you've learned—believe that such an attack isn't really necessary?"

Desmond was the first to lift his hand, followed by Alexander and Hayley Millwright. Isabelle, who was holding Daisy, raised her hand. Vic and Reyna glanced at each other and raised their hands, followed by all five of the wildcards.

Gibson nodded. "You see that? From what we know about the revenge gene, some people have it, some don't." He raised a finger as if he expected to be interrupted. "And here's why this is important. We also know that even if you have this genetic predisposition for revenge, it's not an absolute rule within your personality.

It's a predisposition, not a rule. Many of the research subjects eventually set aside their grudges and reported they were glad they had. Further studies showed the need for revenge can be so strong that it overrules logic, but often it gradually tapers off until it's little more than a nagging urge. We do not *need* to attack the beings who wish to be our friends. I, for one, would like to continue living."

"The Outlanders didn't destroy eight billion people on your world," Emily said. "Who the hell are you to tell us we shouldn't want revenge?"

"That's just it!" Gibson replied. "Our studies found that more heinous crimes resulted in more frequent triggering of the revenge gene, as well as a higher level of determination to carry out acts of violent revenge. The RHF pandemic resulted in suffering beyond anything our people had previously experienced. But you guys... holy hell, what happened to you guys is off the charts. It's beyond any of our experiences—beyond anything humans have *ever* experienced. Not surprisingly, your determination to carry out violence is likewise off the charts. I'm suggesting that we give this some time."

Xavier stepped away from Celia. "And I have a suggestion for you." He took a swing at Gibson.

Gibson saw it coming and easily blocked the fist with his forearm. "You don't want to tangle with me, pal. I'm just trying to save this colony."

"I've heard enough," Infinity said. "Gibson, you've made your point, but I personally don't give a shit." She glanced around at the migrants who had indicated they understood the importance of wiping out the Outlanders. "We aren't giving Kitty's people the pleasure of making us kiss the feet of the bastards who killed our planet. The sooner we find their settlement, the sooner we can devise a plan. We need the three rifles, and we need the knives, hatchets, and spears. If you're with me, let's get started. If you're not, fine—just stay out of our way."

She turned back toward camp, but Desmond grabbed her elbow. "This isn't like you, Infinity! You can't just—"

She threw her right leg around the back of his knees and took him down with an elbow to his neck. He hit the ground hard, his eyes wide with surprise.

She glared down at him. "Maybe we don't know each other as well as we thought!" She hesitated only a moment before she turned and headed for camp.

12
____

PURSUIT

MAY 3 - 7:47 AM

GIBSON EXTENDED A HAND. Desmond accepted it and allowed the wildcard to pull him to his feet. He looked up the hillside. Infinity along with those who apparently shared her fixation on revenge were hiking steadily up the slope. She hadn't even glanced back.

Gibson released Desmond's hand and gazed up the hill. "You realize we have to stop them, right?"

Desmond rubbed his throat where Infinity had elbowed him. "They're not exactly eager to listen to reason."

"That's true, but we still have to stop them. My mates and I didn't volunteer for this endeavor just to be slaughtered by cloned aliens."

"I can't believe it," Isabelle said. Daisy was starting to whimper and squirm in her arms. "Lenny didn't even look at me after I voted against him. He didn't even look at Daisy."

Hayley put a hand on the back of her daughter's neck. "Give

me a chance to talk to them. They aren't thinking clearly right now, but maybe I can get through to them." She took her husband's hand and the two headed up the slope.

"I don't think this is going to end well," Tessa said.

Sue added, "There's going to be violence—either in our own group or with those Outlanders."

Gibson turned to them sharply. "If all you have is pessimism, maybe you should shut the hell up."

The two women looked down at the ground, while Latonya and Donica averted their eyes.

"Jesus," said Vic, "you wildcards are fine pieces of work."

Desmond sighed and started up the hill. He struggled to make sense of the recent developments. Just this morning everything seemed to be going well. Now the whole colony was splitting apart, and its future was uncertain at best. Most disturbing of all, though, was the look he'd seen in Infinity's eyes. At this moment he should have been focusing on strategies for preventing the upcoming conflict, but her face was all he could think about. She had seemed so incensed, so outraged. Even worse, she obviously felt deep disappointment in Desmond, as if he had betrayed her.

By the time Desmond arrived at the camp, Infinity already had taken the three rifles from the Outlanders' shelter. She was studying the controls of one of the weapons, impatiently pushing and pulling on things as she pointed the device's muzzle toward the boxes assembled on the front of the bunker. Desmond stepped up beside her. He eyed the rifle in her hand as well as the two on the ground by her feet.

She glanced at him. "Don't even think of touching those. We need all three." She pushed her finger into a hole on the gun's grip, and an almost silent *pfft* came from the weapon's muzzle. "That's how the damn thing works," she muttered. She aimed the rifle at a specific spot in the boxes and fired again. *Pfft.*

She picked up the two spare rifles, as if she didn't trust Desmond to leave them alone, and strode to the bunker.

Desmond wasn't sure what to say, so he simply followed.

She put her finger on a small hole in one of the boxes, confirming where the projectile had passed through. She tucked the three weapons against her side and ducked into the bunker.

Desmond ducked in behind her.

The projectile had cleanly passed through both sides of the box.

"Are we going to talk about this?" Desmond asked.

Infinity moved to the rear of the bunker and found a corresponding hole in the rock face. "Good," she muttered as she touched the hole. Then she glanced at Desmond. "All I want to hear is that you're with me on this. If you're not, there's nothing to say." She started to duck back out of the bunker.

"I've always been with you on everything, Infinity. Maybe I could even be with you on this. But this is really, really important, and it's dangerous. It requires careful analysis."

She rose back up to her full height. "You're right. You've always been with me on everything. Now you're not. Analysis done." She ducked out and left him standing alone.

When Desmond exited the bunker, Hayley was earnestly addressing some of the group, but no one was paying her much attention. Emily and Steven had gathered some of the knives and hatchets and were zipping them into a small backpack. Gideon and Lenny were each holding four spears, two in each hand, and were standing there as if they were impatient to get going.

Hayley continued talking. "It's our duty to contemplate what this colony represents. We are among the last human beings from our Earth. The last, out of billions! This is a responsibility not to be taken lightly. I think we can all agree that we should carefully consider—as a group—any decisions that might affect our future here."

"Our future?" Infinity demanded. "We have no future unless we have self-respect. We need to have pride in who we are and what we've done. We've been put here to help Kitty's people start an Outlander civilization, don't you get that? It's not going to happen!"

Out of the corner of his eye, Desmond saw Gibson motion to his mates. The five wildcards moved into a line, blocking Infinity and the others from heading west. "We can't let you leave this camp right now," Gibson said.

Infinity handed one of the rifles to Gideon and one to Emily, then she leveled the third at Gibson. "I've wasted two bullets figuring out how this thing works. I guess I don't mind wasting five more clearing our path. You have three seconds."

Gibson narrowed his eyes, but within only a second he started moving to the side. "Let them pass," he said to his mates. They moved aside with him.

Infinity turned to Desmond and studied him.

"Please, Infinity, stay here," he said, struggling to keep his voice from breaking.

She pursed her lips. The lines around her eyes might have indicated an intense sadness, but Desmond couldn't be sure.

Reyna spoke up for the first time. "You can't possibly kill all the Outlanders. You know that, don't you?"

Vic added, "You'll be lucky to even kill one."

"Maybe so," said Infinity. "At least we'll show Kitty and her people we're not going to be what they want us to be."

Armando stepped forward. He was holding the only two walkie talkies the migrants had brought with them to this world. He held one out to Infinity. "I want you to take this, kiddo. You know I can't go with you. I'd slow you down, and I'd be useless anyway. What I can do is be available if you need to talk. Please take it."

Infinity took the device and slipped it into the pocket of her shorts. She turned and headed west, pointing her rifle at Gibson as she passed by the wildcards.

Behind her, Gideon, Lenny, Xavier, Richard, Poppy, Emily, and Steven followed. Xavier glanced over his shoulder once and gave a confident nod to Celia, but Lenny didn't even look back at Isabelle and Daisy.

———

DESMOND KICKED a stone and watched it clatter over the rocky bluff and come to a stop fifteen feet below. Everything had fallen apart in less than two hours. Perhaps if he'd handled things differently Infinity would still be in camp. Maybe if he'd broken the news to the others in a different way, perhaps starting with the reasoning that Fisher, Hero, Bard, and any others of their kind could not be held accountable for crimes committed by their distant ancestors. Just like Daisy couldn't be blamed for Lenny's or Isabelle's transgressions.

On the beach, Desmond himself had almost succumbed to a fit of violent rage, and he was inherently a nonviolent person. He should have known Infinity and some of the others might have a stronger reaction than what he'd experienced. He kicked another rock over the bluff. Why couldn't he have handled things differently?

Gibson's voice came from the west end of camp. "Desmond! If you're done sulking, we need you over here."

Desmond suppressed a curse and made his way to the others. All the migrants who remained in camp were now gathered around the wildcards, including Celia and Armando, both of whom had made it clear they favored attacking the Outlanders.

Gibson waited for Desmond to join the group and said, "You know what we need to do, and we're wasting our time standing around. We have to stop the others from doing something stupid resulting in disaster for all of us."

"And how do you propose we do that?" Desmond asked, although he knew exactly what Gibson meant.

Gibson tilted his head to the side and frowned, apparently refusing to state the obvious.

Armando spoke up. "I do not condone violence within our own group. It's counterproductive."

Gibson shot Armando a look. "And yet you condone attacking the Outlanders, which is a suicide move. How is that not counterproductive?"

Armando shook his head. "I could see at the time that many of our people desperately needed some form of retribution—or at least to go through the motions of seeking retribution. Perhaps I need it myself. I support their efforts, but honestly I'm hoping they ultimately discover bringing their aggression to full fruition is impractical." He held up the walkie-talkie he'd kept. "Perhaps she will be inclined to seek my counsel, allowing me to temper her inclination for aggression."

Armando glanced at Desmond with a grim face. Desmond felt a pang of compassion for the older man. He also felt a bit of guilt. Armando had supported Infinity, even knowing her motives were self-destructive, whereas Desmond had done nothing but question and condemn her.

Celia said, "Do you all really think it matters that these particular Outlanders aren't the ones who killed everyone? It doesn't. Any beings capable of doing such a thing cannot be allowed to exist. It's as simple as that."

"By that logic," retorted Isabelle, "we should have tried to kill Kitty and her companions. How well do you think that would have gone over?"

"Enough of this horseshit!" Gibson shouted. "We're wasting time. My mates and I, we're going after the others. One way or another, we'll stop this insanity." His eyes met Desmond's. "If you want to accomplish that without violence, then you'd better come with us." He looked around at the others. "The same goes for the rest of you. Jesus! If this colony didn't bicker like a bunch of goddamn monkey-frogs, we wouldn't be in this mess in the first place."

Vic stepped toward Gibson. "I gladly take orders from Des and from Infinity. You know why? They've earned my respect. I ain't seen no reason why I should respect you or your harem."

Desmond raised both his hands. "Alright! As much as I question Gibson's attitude and philosophies, he's actually making some sense right now. We probably should try to catch up with Infinity and the others. Maybe we can still talk them out of attacking the Outlanders. Maybe they're already starting to realize this is a mistake, and we can persuade them to come back to camp." Desmond eyed Vic. "Okay?"

Vic turned to Reyna. "I'm gonna need you to stay here, babe." She nodded, and Vic turned back to Desmond. "Yep, I'm coming with you."

<hr>

TEN MINUTES LATER, Desmond, Vic, and the five wildcards headed west. Desmond wore a backpack containing a water filter, an empty water bladder, a first aid kit, and the only hatchet Infinity's group hadn't taken. Vic and the wildcards each had a general-purpose hunting knife. In addition, Sue and Donica carried the two spears that had been left behind. Desmond had no intention of using the weapons on Infinity, or any other humans for that matter, but he wanted his group to be prepared for any possible danger. Hopefully they wouldn't be gone more than a few hours.

Those remaining behind included Armando, Celia, Reyna, Hayley and Alexander Millwright, Isabelle, and Daisy. Desmond was still concerned about the effects of Hero's kick on Celia's baby. Because the two doctors were now gone, Armando and the others had promised they'd keep an eye on her and make her rest.

As Desmond and his team headed away from camp, he could still hear Celia ranting about how the Outlanders had to pay for what their species had done. He also heard Armando speaking on the walkie talkie, alerting Infinity that Desmond's group was leaving camp with the goal of preventing her attack on the Outlanders. Desmond decided this warning probably didn't matter. If anything, it might give Armando an opportunity to reason with her.

The group headed downhill and decided to make their way along the beach, based on the assumption that the Outlanders' apparent affinity for water would mean their city would be somewhere on or near the shore. Desmond figured Infinity would make the same assumption. After wading through the narrow swamp, they emerged onto the beach and soon came upon multiple sets of human footprints in the sand—Infinity's team.

They followed the footprints on the beach for a mile or so, and it became obvious that the shoreline was curving to the south. Numerous islands were visible offshore, and it occurred to Desmond that he and the other migrants were probably on an island similar to all the others. He silently hoped to discover the Outlander city was actually situated on one of the other islands. This would prevent Infinity and her team from carrying out an attack, at least for the time being.

After another half mile, a massive sea cliff stopped their progress. The relatively flat beach ended abruptly at the base of a nearly vertical rock face some fifty yards tall, which extended at least a hundred yards out into the sea. The footprints revealed that Infinity's team had turned here and headed off the beach and into the forest, probably determined to hike south to find a place where they could climb over the hill and continue west.

Desmond paused and wiped sea spray and sweat from his face. He pressed two fingers to his forearm and pulled them back. His fingers left pale impressions for a second or so, indicating he was already getting sunburned. He was glad he'd be moving into the shade of the forest.

"Hey guys, check that out," said Donica. She was pointing out to sea, beyond the edge of the cliff.

Desmond shaded his eyes and squinted. About a mile offshore to the northwest stood an artificial structure. The object was a light shade of tan, and its overall shape resembled a bulbous water tower, with a single thick support in the center surrounded by thinner supports near the perimeter. Rather than having a smooth exterior, the outer surface was dotted with pill-shaped pods the same color as the main body. From this distance, judging the structure's size was difficult, but Desmond guessed it stood at least 150 feet above the water's surface, which would make each of the attached pods about twenty feet wide and ten feet tall.

"Do you think that's the Outlander's city?" Tessa asked.

"That ain't no city," Vic replied. "Looks to me like a building that serves a specific purpose. So, yeah, it might be *part* of a city, but only one part."

"Then their city must be damn large," Gibson said. "Far too large for a handful of humans to think they could invade it and kill all the residents. It's a fool's errand."

Desmond stared at the offshore structure. "Hero told us Kitty's people left behind a production factory, which the Outlanders use to produce materials needed to build their city. Maybe that's the factory?"

"I'd buy that before I'd believe that's the city itself," Vic said.

Gibson shuffled his feet in the sand impatiently. "So, it's likely the city is located on the shore, maybe just on the other side of this cliff. We need to catch up to the others before they get there. Let's quit standing around yapping."

Desmond gazed at Gibson for a moment. "Before we go any farther, I need to know you're not going to try to hurt the other members of our colony. There are only twenty-two of us, which means every person is immensely valuable."

Gibson returned his gaze without wavering. "You plan to sweet talk them into turning around and coming back?"

"*Every* person is valuable," Desmond repeated. "No violence!"

Gibson's face was as rigid as stone. "You're the boss. Now, can we go?"

Vic took a step toward Gibson. "Are you done being a dick?"

The wildcard held both his hands up as if surrendering. "I'm on your side, remember?"

"There are no sides," Desmond said. "We're all in this together. Including the Outlanders. We're going to catch up with Infinity's group and convince them to at least wait before they decide to do something which will drastically affect the entire group. Does everyone understand?"

They all nodded, and without another word Desmond led the group away. He followed the footprints to where they disappeared into the forest at the base of the cliff.

"I don't see no swamp here," Vic said. "At least we don't gotta slog through the muck again."

They made their way inland. Vic had been right—the ground was dry here, but the forest understory was thicker, forcing them to skirt around numerous clumps of vines and brush. At about a quarter mile south of the beach, the sheer cliff began to transition into a steep, forested hillside and then eventually into a traversable slope.

Desmond hadn't seen any signs of Infinity's group since leaving the beach, but it seemed logical she would have started up the hill as soon as she had found a reasonable path. The hillside was even more tangled with vegetation than the flat area at its base, so he kept moving south until he found an opening in the brush that appeared to be an animal trail. He turned and led the others up the hillside.

Whatever animals had been moving through here must have been larger than humans, as the trail was a good four feet wide. Perhaps this was a travel corridor used by Outlanders riding their frog-steeds. If so, this could be a good thing or a very bad thing.

The trail continued up the hill to the west, occasionally winding back and forth around rocky outcrops. Finally, the surrounding vegetation became sparse as the slope began to level out, then it became little more than a grassy meadow that covered the hill's domed peak. Even here the trail was worn and easy to follow. It continued on directly over the hill's grassy dome, disappearing on the other side. Although he could detect no human footprints, Desmond figured there was a reasonable chance Infinity's team had taken this same path. He pushed on, still panting heavily from the climb. The others followed without protest.

Desmond hiked until he could see over the hill's peak to the west side of the meadow and beyond. Two sights brought him to a stop. First, about eighty yards ahead, a herd of creatures grazed on the grassy west slope. They had the same basic body shape as the Outlanders' frog-steeds, but these creatures were even larger, perhaps eight hundred pounds each. Second, far beyond the herd, arranged over the water and on the adjoining beach, was a network of structures that could only be the Outlanders' city.

"Damn, would you look at that," Vic said as he stopped at Desmond's side. "That's got to be the city. But it ain't no city at all. If those things are dwellings, there can't be more than fifty of them. That ain't nothing but a village."

The *things* Vic was referring to were more pill-shaped pods, arranged in a seemingly random fashion on and within a network of support beams and elevated sidewalks. None of the pods actually touched the sea or the beach. Instead, they were affixed to the framework at varying heights, about twenty feet to at least a hundred feet above the sand or water. Interspersed throughout the tan-colored pods and framework were various objects of different colors, unidentifiable at this distance. A few figures could be seen walking about, although they were too far away for Desmond to be sure they were Outlanders. Two dark, elongated objects floated alongside some of the supports at the oceanside base of the framework—whale submarines.

He shifted his gaze to the teardrop-shaped structure about a mile out to sea. Although it was the same color as the framework straddling the surf and beach, the offshore structure was more symmetrical, perhaps more human-like in design. It was starting to make sense. Kitty's people had designed the production factory, and the Outlanders had created their framework city, apparently using building materials manufactured in the factory.

"This isn't what I was hoping to see," said Gibson after he and the other wildcards had come to a stop and studied the scene for a moment.

Desmond glanced at the herd of creatures. They were moving from north to south across the trail with their heads down, apparently grazing on the vegetation or rooting for grubs or other small animals. "Why's that?" he asked Gibson, even though he was pretty sure of the answer.

"Because it's small. There can't be more than a few hundred of them living there. Probably far fewer. If I were planning to attack the Outlanders, I'd be encouraged and emboldened by what I'm looking at right now."

Desmond studied the framework of pods. Would Infinity actually believe she and only six other humans had a chance of raiding that structure without immediately being slaughtered? Even if there were only fifty Outlanders, it would be suicide. Even just twenty would be bad. Then he recalled the outrage and determination etched into Infinity's expression as she'd been preparing to leave him behind for this insane mission.

He turned to Vic and the wildcards. "Gibson's probably right. I was hoping Infinity would find a much larger city then simply give up and return to camp. But if this is the entire city, it's smaller than expected. I agree they still might be determined to go through with it."

Desmond turned back to the west. The creatures were still blocking the trail, so he headed north to give them a wide berth.

As the humans moved over the hill's peak, they became fully exposed. One of the grazing beasts straightened its front legs, lifted its head from the ground, and stared. Then it opened its mouth and let out a sound somewhere between a burp and a bark. The others abruptly raised up as well.

"Just move slowly," Desmond said. "Grazing animals aren't usually aggressive unless they feel threatened."

One of the creatures burped and began galloping straight for the humans. A split second later, the entire herd charged after it, quickly gaining speed.

"Oh shit," Tessa said. "Stand our ground or run?"

The herd was closing in fast. Desmond swung around and scanned the area. The nearest trees were down the slope to the west. Too far away. "Stand your ground! Bunch up together."

Cursing, the others huddled up beside him.

Desmond raised his hands. "Put your arms up to look bigger. Don't even try to use your weapons."

Everyone extended their arms.

"It ain't working," Vic said, his voice strangely calm.

Vic was right. The herd wasn't slowing down. There were at least twelve of them, running full speed, their feet pounding the ground. Thirty yards. Twenty. Ten.

The creatures plowed into the humans.

Desmond's head slammed into someone's face behind him, then the group tumbled over each other, screaming and grunting. Legs and arms flailed wildly, and either an elbow or a knee caught

Desmond's face, crushing his nose, the pain momentarily blinding him.

"Get up and run!" Gibson shouted.

Desmond blinked several times to get past the pain and started to get to his feet, only to be knocked over again by something massive. The creature stuck its wet, grunting snout under his side, as if it were trying to root in the ground beneath him. It then jerked its head up, rolling him violently across the grass. Again, he tried getting up, but the beast repeated the attack, this time actually flipping him several feet into the air and sending him tumbling. As the creature approached him a third time, Desmond glanced around and saw that the other creatures were doing the same thing—rolling and tossing human bodies, violently shoving the cursing, grunting migrants in the same direction.

Again, the beast flipped him before he could get to his feet. And again, tossing him on top of another tumbling body. Beneath him, Tessa let out a pained yelp just before two slobbery snouts rammed into both of them and rolled them over each other as if they were now a single multi-limbed rag doll.

Relentlessly, like living bulldozers, the creatures shoved and flipped the migrants across the hill's grassy peak. As the ground began to slope downward, the beasts abruptly stopped. They stood shoulder-to-shoulder, snorting and showering the battered humans with slobber.

Desmond hesitated to get up, assuming he'd simply be knocked over again as soon as he tried. He looked around at the others. "Is everyone okay? Any broken bones?"

"Freakin' bruised," Vic said, "but in one piece."

"I think I'm okay," Sue said. "Just shaken up."

The others indicated that they weren't injured too badly.

The massive frog-like beasts stood their ground, almost like they were daring the migrants to try to get up.

"Maybe we can slowly crawl away," Gibson suggested. "No sudden movements."

No one seemed to have a better idea, so they all got to their hands and knees and crawled down the slope. The nearest trees were still at least fifty yards away.

The creatures stayed put, still snorting.

Desmond cautiously got to his feet when the group was about twenty yards from the line of beasts. The others followed his lead, staying in a low crouch.

The creatures didn't charge, so Desmond rose to his full height. Now he could see over the animals' brawny shoulders. Behind them, back where the humans had first been knocked to the ground, five juvenile frog-beasts stood huddled together, each of them about the size of a Labrador retriever.

"Well, that explains a lot," he muttered to no one in particular.

The humans backed away until they had entered the forest on the hill's west slope, at which point Desmond finally allowed himself to breathe normally. He turned to the others and carefully looked them over. They were covered with dirt, grass stains, and animal slobber. Most of them were still staring up at the frog-beasts, wide-eyed and shell-shocked.

"That could've gone worse," Gibson said. "But it also could've gone a hell of a lot better."

13

____

ENCOUNTER

MAY 3 - 10:50 AM

INFINITY GAZED out over an open pasture where a half dozen Outlander frog-steeds milled about, occasionally chasing and nipping at each other. Although similar in basic shape, these frog-steeds were clearly a different species from the more massive creatures her team had seen as they crossed the open ground atop the hill behind her. Those creatures had acted aggressively, forcing her group to take a detour around the herd while remaining within the forest, circling to the south around the grassy hilltop.

The frog-steeds before her now paused only briefly upon spotting the humans and then went back to business as usual. Infinity's team crouched behind a cluster of low vegetation as they took in the scene.

It wasn't the frog-steeds that interested her so much as what lay beyond the pasture. To the north a gap in the forest revealed a path to the beach. Framed within the gap was the bizarre structure her group had spotted from atop the hill, a collection of egg-like containers or dwellings situated in no particular arrangement on a framework of supports. This had to be what the Outlanders had referred to as their city, but it was nothing more than a village.

Infinity wished Desmond was with her. He would see that attacking the Outlanders might not be suicidal after all. Thinking about Desmond triggered a dull ache throughout her body. Why couldn't he understand how important this was? How could he think she was capable of coexisting with these planet killers? It was unthinkable, and now she was sickened by the knowledge that she might die today without Desmond at her side. They should be doing this together, goddammit.

"What do you guys think?" Gideon asked. He was crouched beside Infinity, looking across the pasture at the village.

"I don't see us simply storming the place," Emily said. "It's elevated, and it looks like we'd have to move single-file on those walkways. If they have any concept of self defense, which we know they do, they could easily hold us off. Probably just pick us off one-by-one with their rifles."

Infinity dropped to her knees to stay out of sight behind the brush and gestured for the others to do the same. "Our best chance is to deal with them one at a time. Two or three at the most. Ambush them as they leave the village. If more than three are in a group, we stay hidden. If there are three or less, we use these." She gestured to the rifles at her feet. "Three of us will use a verbal signal to fire simultaneously. When they go down, three others rush in and finish them with hatchets. When the dead ones fail to return to the village, more will come out to look for them, and we do it all over again."

Infinity noticed Richard and Poppy frowning at each other. "You two having second thoughts?"

They hesitated, then Poppy said, "We were talking on the trek here. Infinity, we agree with you. We shouldn't be forced to live as stewards or attendants—let alone friends—to the Outlanders. We can't imagine ever becoming comfortable with such an arrangement."

Infinity raised her brows. "But?"

"But perhaps there's another way," Richard said. "What if we moved our camp far from here? We could simply live in isolation, perhaps never even encountering the Outlanders. Yes, maybe this island is no larger than all the others we've observed offshore, but surely it's large enough. Or maybe we can get to one of the other islands, and then we'd have it all to ourselves."

She shook her head. "Kitty made it clear our purpose was to become friends. She'll either kill us or destroy this entire—"

"We didn't mean all of us," Poppy interjected. "The others back at camp still want to follow Kitty's orders. They can become friends with the Outlanders, keeping Kitty happy, and we can live our own lives without suffering endless mental anguish."

Infinity stared at the two doctors. She actually hadn't thought of this. It would require two things that were still impossible. First, this wasn't any different from being friends with the Outlanders. Letting them live was the same as forgiving them. Second, how could she possibly exist so near Desmond and not have him in her life? She looked from one migrant's face to the next. Richard and Poppy were in agreement, and they'd remain together. Same with Emily and Steven. Celia wasn't physically here with Xavier, but she was with him in spirit. She'd remain at his side. And Gideon didn't have a partner at all.

Her gaze fell upon Lenny, and their eyes met. Isabelle, like Desmond, didn't understand why this mission was so important.

The lines on Lenny's face at this moment were deeper than Infinity had ever seen them before. He was suffering inside, the same as she was. He slowly shook his head as if understanding what she was thinking. "I don't know, Infinity. Maybe there *is* a better way to deal with this."

She closed her eyes and inhaled deeply, trying to think. She wished she could use one of the meditation techniques she'd relied on over the years, but there simply wasn't time for that now.

Steven spoke up. "We're not seriously going to sit around here and talk ourselves out of this, are we?"

Infinity opened her eyes.

Steven started getting to his feet. "I, for one, am *not* having second thoughts." He rose to his full height and turned to look out over the pasture. His eyes narrowed and he snapped his head around toward Infinity. "Shit! We've got comp—"

Something squirted out the side of Steven's forehead. His face went blank and his knees buckled. He collapsed. His arms and legs began to spasm.

Infinity stared at her friend for only a second or so before realizing he was dead. "Grab your weapons!" she hissed.

"Steven!" Emily cried.

Infinity wanted to command Emily to be quiet, but she doubted it would work, so instead she snatched one of the rifles and aimed it through the brush. She couldn't see anything, so she lowered herself until she was flat on her belly. From there, a gap in the undergrowth gave her a better view. She could see two Outlanders on frog-steeds, perhaps thirty yards away, both of them aiming weapons toward the hidden humans.

"Oh my God," Emily sobbed.

Infinity turned to Emily with a finger pressed to her lips, but Emily wasn't looking. Instead, she was grabbing one of the rifles. She fumbled with the holes and levers, but Infinity hadn't taken the time yet to show the others how to use the devices.

"Emily!" Infinity whispered.

"Shit!" Emily growled as she stared at the weapon in her hands. She dropped it, grabbed one of the hatchets out of the pack beside her, and lunged directly into the thick vegetation between the humans and the Outlanders, thrashing her way through it and cursing the whole time.

Infinity gritted her teeth, lowered her head again, and stared down her weapon's sights at the Outlanders. Both were still aiming at the bushes, perhaps waiting for a clear shot or for Emily to stop moving.

Infinity heard the others behind her cursing and getting to their feet. She ignored all distractions and concentrated on aiming. Her fingertip found the hole on the side of the gun's grip. She held her breath, sighting in on one of the Outlander's heads, and slipped her finger into the hole.

Pfft.

The being's head jerked slightly. His weapon slipped from his hands and fell to the ground. Infinity didn't wait to see if the being was incapacitated. She shifted the rifle to aim at the other Outlander, who seemed momentarily distracted by his wounded companion. At that moment, Emily broke free of the brush and charged, shrieking like an animal.

Infinity tried sighting in on the Outlander, but now Emily was blocking her shot. She grunted and got to her knees and then to her feet. When she rose above the brush, she saw a third Outlander who hadn't been visible before. She also saw all five of the other migrants charging forward with Emily, quickly closing in on the two remaining beings, both of whom were now aiming at their attackers.

Infinity snapped the rifle to her shoulder, chose the Outlander on the right, and quickly fired a shot at its chest. She swiveled to the Outlander on the left just in time to see Emily collapse and plow face first into the ground.

The migrants closed the last few yards of distance, swinging hatchets and knifes, hacking the Outlanders and their steeds. The steeds tried biting and kicking, only to have their faces slashed repeatedly, causing them to rear back, dumping their riders. Without hesitating, Xavier and Lenny leapt on one of the Outlanders while Gideon, Richard, and Poppy attacked the other.

The humans chopped and stabbed the beings ruthlessly, sending chunks of flesh and droplets of fluid into the air with every swing.

Seconds later, the fight was over. The three Outlanders lay dead on the ground, while one of their steeds stood several yards away, wavering on its feet and bleeding profusely from its face and neck. The other two steeds had escaped and were now standing with the herd out in the center of the meadow, watching the humans warily.

Infinity scrambled over to Steven and tilted his head to one side and then the other. There was a clean entrance hole in his right temple and a gory exit hole in his left, still oozing gray brain matter and blood. He was dead. She leapt up and ran around the thick brush to join the others, who had gathered beside Emily. Infinity knelt down to feel for a pulse.

"You don't need to bother," Gideon said, his words measured and ominous. "The bastards killed her."

Infinity checked anyway. The first thing she saw was a gory exit wound on the back of Emily's neck. She rolled Emily over. The projectile had entered just below her chin. She felt Emily's neck for a pulse but only felt dead flesh. "Goddammit!" Infinity muttered.

A scuffling sound prompted her to straighten up. Lenny and Xavier were dragging one of the hacked-up Outlanders toward the trees, leaving behind a trail of rusty-brown stains on the dirt and grass.

Lenny paused and eyed Infinity. "We gotta get them hidden before another group comes riding through here."

"They're right," said Gideon. He pulled Emily up by her arms and smoothly hefted her body onto his shoulders. He shot Infinity a grim look and carried Emily to the trees.

Richard and Poppy started dragging another Outlander body.

Infinity scanned the meadow from one end to the other. No new Outlanders yet. She looked through the gap at the strange framework and its egg-like dwellings. Nothing alarming there, at least nothing she could see from this distance. A bubbling huff came from her left, and she turned to see the injured steed collapse onto its belly. Its head was up, and it was watching her, although one of its eyes appeared to be missing.

Infinity moved to the third dead Outlander, the one she'd shot in the head. The being was lying face down, his two long legs extended loosely to their full length in the grass. His double tail had somehow looped several times around one of his legs.

The Outlander didn't look so dangerous now. But these things —at least their genetic ancestors—were the worst kind of evil. Infinity found it comforting that they were mortal and could be killed so easily.

Again, she looked out at the Outlanders' village—their city. If allowed to proliferate, these beings would become evil all over again, wouldn't they? That had been part of Infinity's reasoning for planning an attack. But now, standing over the Outlander she'd killed, she wasn't so sure.

What if Desmond and the others had been right? What if she had a genetic tendency to fixate on revenge? Maybe she did have some supposed revenge gene. Perhaps given enough time, she could forgive these beings.

She sighed and picked up the Outlander's dropped rifle. The truth was, none of that even mattered now. Her team had killed three Outlanders, and this course of action was a one-way street. The war had already begun.

Lenny stepped up beside her and gazed down at the alien body. He gripped two of the long toes on the Outlander's right foot then glanced up at her. "Grab a leg. Let's get this sack of bones out of sight."

"Hold on," she said. She carried the rifle over to the dying frog-steed. The creature, now barely able to hold its head up, watched her with its remaining eye.

Infinity said, "You're innocent in all of this, aren't you? Kind of like the people of my world were." She leaned to the side slightly and looked at the creature's massive body. "And you're going to be a bitch to drag."

She held the rifle's muzzle to the beast's forehead and inserted her finger into the hole on the grip.

14

FACEOFF

MAY 3 - 11:36 AM

DESMOND WIPED his nose and mouth, and his hand came away covered in blood. He'd forgotten about the blow to his face. His nose was tender, perhaps broken, but there wasn't much he could do about it now. He insisted the migrants check themselves over for broken bones or cuts that might need antiseptic. He left the trees and cautiously made his way back to the spot where his group had first been knocked to the ground. The herd of frog-beasts had moved off to the south, but he kept his body low to avoid pissing them off again.

Miraculously, the pack containing the first aid kit, hatchet, and water filter was still on his back, but he wanted to retrieve the two spears the others had dropped. The spears were there, although one of them had been snapped in half. On the ground near the good spear was one of the hunting knives, still in its plastic sheath. He grabbed the spear and knife and returned to his team.

"I think we're all okay, but you look like hell," Vic said, nodding toward Desmond's face.

Desmond wiped his nose again. Fresh blood was still flowing, and now it covered a good portion of the front of his shirt. He shrugged, dismissing it. "If everyone's in one piece, I suggest we get moving. The others are probably devising a plan as we speak."

"What if we can't convince them to come back with us?" Tessa asked.

Desmond handed the spear and knife to Donica. "We'll convince them."

"What if we can't?"

"We'll worry about that when and if it happens."

"Shouldn't we have a plan?"

Desmond cursed under his breath. "We *do* have a plan—convince them not to attack the Outlanders!"

The wildcards exchanged frowns.

"Sounds like a plan to me," Vic said. "Let's get it done."

Desmond turned and headed down the forested slope toward the Outlanders' city. He heard the others following him soon after.

<hr>

An open field lay before Desmond and his team. A herd of Outlander frog-steeds milled about at the west edge of the field, and the city's framework was visible to the north. Now that Desmond was on level ground, he realized the city was taller than he'd previously estimated. The highest of the pill-shaped pods had to be close to three hundred feet above the beach. Apparently, the Outlanders were as comfortable with heights as they were with swimming in the predator-infested sea.

Infinity and her team had to be somewhere in the area. The open field extended almost to the beach, ending in a narrow gap in the forest leading to the city's framework structure. It seemed logical that Outlanders leaving the city would either go east or west on the beach or would enter this field. Infinity would assume the same thing. If she intended to observe the Outlanders' pattern of movement, she'd either be near the beach or somewhere on the perimeter of the field, probably on the eastern side since they'd come from that direction. He turned to his team and explained this reasoning. No one disagreed.

"I see two choices," he said. "We can work our way through the forest around the east side of the field until we find them. That way we'd stay more or less hidden from the Outlanders. Or we can walk the field out in the open. That way we might be spotted by Outlanders, but that may not be a bad thing."

"Unless the others have already tried to attack," Gibson said, "in which case they're probably dead, and the Outlanders will shoot us on sight."

Desmond eyed the wildcard. As much as he despised the man's casual mention of Infinity's possible death, Gibson's assessment was probably accurate. "Okay, then we'll stay out of sight." Again, he took off without waiting for the others, hoping they'd hang back and let him lead. He wanted to be the first to confront Infinity and her team.

The forest became thicker, and the understory brush slowed his progress. When he was halfway around the east side of the field, Desmond considered waiting for the others to catch up so he could suggest they walk in the open field instead, but then something gray in the brush ahead caught his eye. He froze, eyeing the object. Whatever it was, it appeared to be covered with freshly-cut tree branches. It wasn't moving, so he cautiously approached.

Vic and the wildcards caught up and stood beside him, They all stared at the object. Desmond pulled away several of the branches, revealing a dead frog-steed. The creature was covered in fresh blood, its face and neck mutilated.

"The Outlanders wouldn't do this to their own steed," Vic said.

"No, they wouldn't," Gibson added. "Which means we're too late. The idiots have already started what they came here to do. The fact that they were able to hide this carcass means they were successful, at least so far."

"Which means we're all screwed," Tessa said.

Desmond scanned the forest around them and spotted another mound of cut branches. His heart began pounding as he approached the spot. He pulled away the branches, revealing not just one but three dead Outlanders, their mangled heads and torsos wet with a brownish liquid, probably their version of blood.

Tessa came up beside him. "Oh, shit, we're *really* screwed."

"There's another," Donica said, pointing.

Desmond turned. He saw a human foot protruding from a smaller pile of severed branches. On the foot was a hiking shoe of the same type issued to all the migrants.

Desmond's heart began pounding even harder, and he fought to control his breathing as he approached the body. The Outlanders had killed one of his friends. Maybe it was even Infinity. The thought made his stomach lurch, and for a moment he feared he might throw up.

He yanked away the branches. The foot belonged to Emily's body. Arranged beside Emily, with one arm draped over her chest, was Steven's body.

Desmond turned to Vic and the wildcards, struggling to contain his emotions. Steven and Emily had been part of his extended family for almost two years. He had grown to care deeply for both of them. Now they were dead. On the other hand, that meant Infinity was still alive.

Or was she? Desmond scanned the forest for signs of a fourth pile of branches. Seeing none, he began systematically circling the area in case one was hidden from view. Vic and the wildcards joined him.

"There ain't nothing else here, brother," Vic said after several minutes of looking. "Maybe we should push on. Let's catch up to them before they all get themselves killed."

Desmond stopped searching. "They can't be far."

"This changes everything," Gibson said. "You know that, right?"

Desmond said, "I know it's not a good situation, but—"

"It changes *everything!*" Gibson said. "I can think of only one way we could prevent these Outlanders from wiping out our entire colony. We have to show them that some of us are on their side— that some of us refuse to allow further attacks on their species."

"That's why we're trying to catch up to Infinity and her group," Desmond said.

Gibson shook his head. "Too late for that. They've already crossed the line. You saw what happened to the people at that other camp. Wiped out—all of them. Our colony's going to suffer the same fate unless we do something drastic."

Desmond stared at the wildcard. "I'm listening."

Gibson waved his hand at the group standing around him. "The seven of us, we go straight to the Outlanders. We surrender and hope they don't immediately kill us. We explain what's happening. We warn them that some of our people are trying to kill them, and we offer to help defend their city."

Desmond considered this. It might actually work. However, it would be a complete betrayal of Infinity and the rest of her team. The Outlanders would probably send out a large group of armed defenders, who would likely track down Infinity's team and kill them. They might even go to the camp and slaughter those who had remained behind.

"I know what you're thinking," Gibson said. "It's too risky to the rest of our colony. Maybe the Outlanders will let them live. We can explain about the revenge gene, and tell them Infinity and the others are temporarily obsessed with retribution. We convince them their desire to attack the Outlanders will eventually fade away. The Outlanders are intelligent beings—surely they'll understand."

Desmond turned to Vic, who was already shaking his head. "Reyna's back at camp," Vic said. "If she were with me now, I might consider it. But she's not."

Desmond turned back to Gibson. "No. We're not doing that."

Gibson narrowed his eyes slightly. "Yes, we are."

Desmond's muscles tensed. "It's too risky for the others. We're not doing it."

Gibson tilted his head toward his four mates. "Maybe you aren't, but we are."

"Gibson's right, and we're with him on this," Tessa said.

Vic stepped forward, fists raised. "I'm gonna enjoy this. Who do I get to knock out first?"

Without warning, Donica thrust out her spear, jabbing Vic in the chest.

"Jesus!" Vic stammered, clutching the puncture wound. Blood was already starting to stain his shirt.

Gibson took a few steps back and signaled for his mates to do the same. All five wildcards stood ready to fight, wielding hunting knives and the spear. "The problem here," Gibson said, his voice low, "is that you guys don't get that we're on your side. You've shown us nothing but disdain since we bridged here. Considering you don't have a better plan, we are now going to the city to beg the Outlanders to understand our colony's situation. It may work. It may not. Maybe they'll kill us all. Maybe they won't kill any of us. Or maybe they'll spare me and my mates and kill the rest of you. To be honest, I'm just about to the point where I'd be okay with that. For the record, I hope they spare all of us. Then maybe you people will finally show us a little respect."

The wildcards backed away, still wielding their weapons, until they were out of the trees. They turned and began walking across the field toward the framework city.

Desmond stepped over to Vic. "You okay, man?"

Blood had spread out beyond Vic's hands and was now making its way down to his waist. "I don't know. I don't know how deep it went." He pulled his shirt up, exposing the wound. "Shit! How bad is it?"

Desmond pushed open the wound with his thumbs, and the cavity immediately filled with blood. "It doesn't look too deep. Probably just into the muscle." He stood back, shrugged off his backpack, and pulled out the first aid kit. "Let's get it cleaned up and stitched."

"Dammit! How'd I let that bitch get the drop on me?"

Desmond got to his knees, unzipped the kit's case, and started sorting through the items inside. He picked out some cleansing wipes and a bottle of antiseptic cream.

"Des, you better check this out."

Desmond glanced up at Vic, who was now staring out into the field. He stood up and followed Vic's gaze. Several hundred yards out into the field, the wildcards had abruptly turned to the right and were now approaching the forest. Desmond saw why—two other people were standing at the forest's edge. He shaded his eyes with his hand and squinted. One of them was Infinity. She was holding an Outlander rifle, pointing it at the ground rather than at the wildcards.

"We better get our asses over there," Vic said.

Desmond dropped the wipes and cream into the case and shoved the kit back into his pack. "Your wound will have to wait." He grabbed the pack and followed Vic out onto the field.

Infinity and the other person with her—it looked like Lenny— were now obviously talking to the wildcards. Gibson's stiff posture and hand gestures indicated that he was becoming agitated.

When they were about a hundred yards out, Infinity turned and saw Desmond and Vic approaching. She must have seen their blood-covered shirts because she promptly lifted the rifle and pointed it at Gibson.

"Oh, crap," Desmond said, and he broke into a run. "Don't shoot!" he shouted. Emily and Steven were already dead, and, as much as he despised Gibson at the moment, the human colony couldn't afford to lose any more members.

Infinity took her eyes off the wildcards and turned to look at Desmond again. This was a mistake. Gibson and the four women rushed forward, taking Infinity and Lenny to the ground among a thrashing pile of fists. Desmond even caught the glint of a knife blade.

Desmond poured on the speed with Vic running at his side. He thrust his hand into his pack, groped around until he found the hatchet, then tossed the pack aside.

Gibson and two of the women were on top of Infinity, swinging punches at her and wrestling to keep her under control. A fist came up and struck Gibson's face, and he let out an enraged curse.

At twenty yards out, Vic pulled ahead of Desmond and ran straight for Lenny, who was engaged in a fierce struggle with Donica and Sue.

"Stop fighting!" Desmond cried.

This had no effect. Gibson was pummeling Infinity as Tessa and Latonya continued trying to restrain her.

At ten yards out, Desmond drew back his hatchet. "Stop!"

Still no effect.

He caught a glimpse of bright red blood in the midst of the struggle—it had to be Infinity's. He was vaguely aware that he shouldn't kill one of his own colony, but the wildcards were attacking Infinity, perhaps even trying to kill her. With only a few steps to go, he grunted and swung the hatchet at Gibson's head.

Gibson's fist came up for another blow.

Without even being aware of his own intent, Desmond reflexively tightened his shoulder muscles, slightly changing the path of the hatchet. The blade caught Gibson's forearm a few inches above the fist with a solid *chonk*.

Gibson's hand flopped to the side, dangling from his arm by a flap of loose skin.

Desmond's momentum carried him into the brawl, his body knocking Gibson and Tessa off of Infinity. He rolled over them and immediately got to his knees, ready to swing the hatchet again.

By the time he glanced at Infinity, she had managed to get her thighs around Latonya's neck and was repeatedly driving hard punches into the woman's face.

Gibson was incapacitated, holding his almost-severed hand and grunting from the pain.

"Don't even try to get up!" Vic commanded.

Desmond turned. The Marine was now standing over Tessa, ready to drive a fist into her head if she attempted to get to her feet. Beyond Vic, Donica and Sue were on the ground, holding their faces and moaning, obviously dazed by blows from Vic. Lenny was sitting up, bleeding from what appeared to be a knife wound on his shoulder.

"Damn, Vic," Lenny said. "Remind me never to get in front of your wicked fist."

Infinity released Latonya, whose face was now beaten bloody. "Dammit, Desmond," she said, getting to her feet, "tell me you didn't bring these wildcards here to kill us."

"Of course not! There wasn't supposed to be any violence. I just wanted to talk you out of attacking the city. Then we found the bodies—Steven and Emily, and the three Outlanders. Things kind of went downhill from there. Infinity, we can't sacrifice our entire colony for the sake of revenge. Or pride."

She glared at him. "It's too late now."

"It's... not... too late," Gibson said, his words punctuated by grunts.

"We can all go together and talk to the Outlanders," Desmond said. "We can convince them that we're not a threat."

Vic snatched a knife from Sue's hand and collected four more that were scattered on the ground.

Infinity continued staring at Desmond. She didn't appear to have any knife wounds. Her face was battered, but Desmond had seen it worse than this on more than one occasion. "We've killed three of them already," she said. "You saw the bodies yourself. It's too late to make friends."

"Where's that damn... first aid kit?" Gibson asked. He was in the process of trying unsuccessfully to get his t-shirt off, probably intending to make it into a tourniquet. "If you're gonna... let me sit here and bleed out... at least let me do what I can to stop it."

Vic stepped over to Gibson and helped him pull the shirt over his head. "Damn sure ought to let you bleed, you bastard, but we can't afford to lose any more of our colony." With one quick motion, Vic ripped the shirt from the neckline to the seam at the waist.

Desmond turned his attention back to Infinity. "It's never too late. That's something I learned from you." He looked around. "Where are the others?"

"They went closer to the city, to assess vulnerabilities." She nodded at Lenny. "We stayed here in case more Outlanders might come by."

"In order to kill them too?"

She nodded, but Desmond detected something in her look—perhaps a hint of uncertainty, or maybe sadness. Whatever it was, it gave him a spark of hope.

"Infinity, are you there?" The voice was Armando's, coming from a small speaker somewhere.

Infinity dug in her pocket and pulled out the walkie talkie Armando had given her. She fumbled with it for a moment and pressed a button. "Yeah, I'm here."

"Thank God you're safe!" came the reply. "There's something of utmost importance I must tell you."

Infinity sighed, and for a moment Desmond thought she might simply put the device back in her pocket. Instead, she pressed the button again and said, "Alright, what is it?"

"Something astounding has happened. Kitty has paid us a visit."

Desmond stepped closer. "What?"

Infinity now appeared to be fully attentive. "Go on, Armando. What happened?"

"She came alone. Walked up from the beach. I happened to be collecting eggs in the swamp when she found me. She asked me how things were going. I felt I had no choice but to tell her what has happened."

Desmond's gut tightened. Infinity glanced up at him and their eyes met. Her expression had faded, and now she simply looked pale.

"Please tell me you have not yet attacked the Outlanders," Armando said.

Infinity blinked once. She pressed the button. "Armando, what did Kitty say to you? What is she going to do?"

"She's not going to do anything as long as we're not a threat to the Outlanders. But she made it abundantly clear there will be consequences if we harm them, or even if we fail to befriend them. Infinity, if we fail, her people will not only destroy us, they will destroy the version of Earth from which we have just bridged—the entire planet. We cannot let that happen. You must abandon all thoughts of retribution."

Infinity's face remained unreadable, as if she were unconscious with her eyes open. She said, "Where is she? Is Kitty coming here?"

"Not that I know of. She listened to what I had to say, gave me her warning, and returned to the beach, presumably to the bridge-in site so she could return to her own version of Earth. Infinity, please return to camp as soon as possible."

She closed her eyes, her brows furrowed. "Okay. Yeah, we'll come back as soon as we can. We have some... some things to deal with here."

"Things to deal with? What kind of—"

She cut him off by pressing the button. "I'll explain when we return, okay? We'll be back as soon as we can." She turned a knob on the walkie talkie until there was a soft click and returned the device to her pocket.

The entire group of battered, bleeding humans remained silent for several long seconds.

Gibson let out another pained grunt as Vic tightened the torn shirt around the wildcard's wrist, cutting off the flow of blood. Gibson's hand was still attached, but it hung loosely by some skin and maybe a few tendons. In spite of his potential life-threatening injury, he spoke up again. "It's not too late. We'll drag the bodies farther into the woods and bury them. The other Outlanders won't know you killed them."

"Lying to them will just make things worse," Desmond said. Then he walked away from the group to retrieve his dropped back-pack. He also hoped the few seconds alone would help him sort out his thoughts. The Outlanders were bound to find out the humans had killed three of their kind. Even if they didn't find out, Kitty's people surely would. Maybe Kitty already knew. Desmond, Infinity, Vic, and Gideon had removed the cameras Kitty's people had inserted into their foreheads to monitor them on the lemur world, but that didn't mean Kitty wasn't still monitoring the humans' actions in some other way. At this point there seemed to be only two choices, and both of them were horrifying. The first choice: Infinity and her team would continue their attempts to kill more Outlanders, resulting in Kitty's people imposing *consequences*. The second choice: Stop the violence, tell the Outlanders what had happened, and hope for the best.

Desmond picked up his pack and returned to the group.

Vic grabbed the pack, pulled out the first aid kit, and kneeled beside Gibson. "We'll probably have to remove the hand and scorch the stump," Vic said to the wildcard, speaking as if he were discussing something as minor as pulling off a stubborn band-aid. "I'll do what I can until Poppy gets here to take over."

Gibson ignored him and spoke to Desmond. "You took my hand, and considering where we are, I may die as a result. I don't blame you for it, though. I'd have done the same thing." The man's face was now pale, and his words were starting to slur.

Desmond didn't know how to respond to this, so he nodded once and turned to Infinity. She was staring toward the Outlander city, her face still without expression. Abruptly, she said, "For better or worse, the shit's about to hit the fan."

"What?" Desmond asked. Then he realized she was still staring, so he followed her gaze.

Outlanders were emerging from the gap leading to the city—at least thirty of them, ambling steadily toward the humans at their full height. Even from this distance, Desmond could see that they each carried a black rifle.

In the midst of the advancing horde, four humans trotted, occasionally stumbling as they tried to keep up. The Outlanders were pulling them along by cords fastened around the humans' necks. Seconds later Desmond recognized them—Xavier, Gideon, Richard, and Poppy.

15

─────────

RETRIBUTION

MAY 3 - 2:40 PM

INFINITY REACHED for the rifle the wildcards had knocked from her hands, but then she hesitated. Picking it up would probably get them all killed.

Donica, Sue, and Latonya were sitting on the ground, nursing their beaten faces, but now they got to their feet. With everyone but Gibson standing, the group turned to face the approaching Outlanders.

Dragging their prisoners with them, the beings strode directly to the humans and stopped. They remained at their full height and pointed their weapons down at Infinity and the others.

Xavier, Gideon, Richard, and Poppy appeared to be unharmed, although the cords around their necks looked uncomfortably tight. Surprisingly, their hands were not bound.

"They were waiting for us," Gideon said. "Somehow they knew we were coming. Took us by surprise."

One of the Outlanders began speaking, pumping his arms

slightly to produce buzzes and clicks. Infinity recognized the shorter tusks and some of his facial features—it was Bard. She then picked out Hero and Fisher amongst the others.

Gideon was standing nearest to Bard, so his translator interpreted the being's words. "I see that you have been hurting each other." Somehow Bard knew the appropriate timing in the translation and directed a finger at several of the migrants, obviously pointing out the blood and wounds. "We have seen this behavior. You kill each other, then you come to kill us. Now that you know we are created from the genetic material of the beings you call Outlanders, you desire retribution. We will not let you kill us."

Desmond spoke up. "We have some things we need to explain. Will you please allow me to explain them to you?" His translator then interpreted his words.

Bard spoke again, and this time Desmond's translator responded. "We sense that three of our kind have died. We believe you have killed them. Is that what you wish to explain?"

Desmond turned to Infinity, frowning, and said, "Well, crap."

The humans fell silent, probably contemplating what to say next, or perhaps waiting for projectiles to pass through their skulls. Infinity had no idea how the Outlanders knew three of their own had been killed, and she didn't really care. Now there was another entire world of humans at stake. Billions of lives. Whether she still wanted to kill the Outlanders or not, she had to try to stop that from happening.

She took a step toward Bard, prompting several rifles to swivel in her direction. "Yes, we want retribution. You should understand why—it's because your genetic ancestors killed everything on our world. If you can't understand how that makes us feel, then you're no better than your ancestors. We came here to attack and kill as many of you as we could, and yes, we did kill three of your people. If you already know about that, then maybe you know that they actually attacked us first. Maybe they knew why we were here and were trying to protect your city. I don't know. Still, they attacked us. They killed two of our people first. Did you know that?"

She paused, waiting for her translator to interpret.

"I'm not sure this is the best approach," Desmond said.

She glanced at him. "Let me finish what I need to say. Then, if they don't kill us, you can have your chance."

The translation ended, and Bard replied. "No, we did not know that."

Infinity went on. "You should consider how you would feel if you were in our shoes... I mean, if you were us. It's impossible for us to not have thoughts of retribution. Some of us aren't even capable of suppressing our desire to carry out retribution. This actually may be in our genetic material."

She paused again, waiting. When her wrist translator fell silent, the Outlanders didn't speak, so she continued. "But there's one need we have that is even stronger than the desire for retribution. It's our need for absolution. Your genetic ancestors did unthinkable things. They killed entire civilizations. Hell, they're *still* killing civilizations even though they, themselves, probably died out long ago. Because of that, I'm pretty sure you also have a need for absolution. Otherwise, why would you fear retribution so much? You should know that we've also done terrible things. Maybe our desire for retribution is really just part of our need for absolution."

Again, she allowed her translator to catch up before going on. "What I'm trying to say is this—we are the same in a lot of ways. Even though our bodies are different, even though we come from different worlds, we all want absolution. Whether they know it or not, Kitty's people—the black-fur beings—they've given us a chance to find absolution together. I have a question for you. Do you want your civilization to become the same as that of your genetic ances-tors? Do you want to eventually destroy other civilizations?"

Infinity's heart began racing as she waited for the translation and then the response. The Outlanders' reply would make or break her entire argument. It could also result in the slaughter of her colony.

"We believe the Outlanders' acts of destruction to be unjust and unmerited," Bard finally said.

Infinity exhaled. "I'm glad to hear that. As I've said, we have done things we regret. It was our own eagerness to use bridging devices that really destroyed our world. We blame your genetic ancestors, but we also have to accept the blame ourselves. And we don't want to make the same mistakes—or become the same civilization—as before." She paused for the translation.

Bard spoke before she could continue, and Infinity's translator interpreted. "It seems we have much in common after all. It would be wise for you to suggest we coexist. Together our two species could become one civilization—the one we desire rather than the civilizations we regret."

Infinity hardly believed what she'd just heard. She turned to the other migrants, most of whom were staring wide-eyed at her or at Bard.

Infinity turned back to the Outlander. "Yes, that sounds like a good solution. Perhaps it's a way we can both eventually find absolution."

After Infinity's translator interpreted her words, Desmond said, "The problem is, we think the black-fur beings created you because they want you to someday become exactly like your genetic ancestors."

Desmond's translator buzzed and clicked, then the Outlanders turned and spoke to each other for several long minutes. Again, Infinity's heart began to pound. This conversation could turn in the wrong direction at any moment.

Bard eyed Desmond and spoke. "The black-fur beings created us. They left us a production factory and taught us many things so we could live and flourish here. But they did not tell us they wish for our civilization to become anything other than what we wish it to become."

Desmond turned to Infinity. He was actually smiling. "You're absolutely brilliant."

She didn't consider herself brilliant at all. She was the same as anyone else—she wanted absolution for her sins. Just hours before, it seemed the only path was revenge. Now she saw a better path, a path that actually resulted in survival of those she cared about. Instead of wiping out the Outlanders, her colony could grow with them, evolve with them, and most importantly, make sure they never became beings eager to destroy others. In this way she and her fellow migrants would be saving rather than annihilating civilizations.

She spoke to Bard. "Are you saying you're willing to do this? You're willing to let us live?"

"The black-fur beings sent you here. We believe the black-fur beings had a good reason for sending you here. We understand that you desire retribution. Now you have had enough retribution, for you have killed three of our kind. Do you believe you have had enough retribution?"

After the translation, Bard waited. Did the being actually expect her to answer this? She glanced at Desmond. He was also waiting for her, his brows raised. "Yes, we've had enough retribution," she said to Bard. It would be suicidal to say otherwise.

Bard spoke again, and Infinity's translator said, "We are pleased that you have had enough retribution. We are pleased that we will not have to kill all of you. Now we only need to kill one of you. If you wish, you may choose the one we must kill."

Infinity glanced down at her translator. Had the device made a mistake? As far as she knew, it hadn't failed before. "Did you just say you need to *kill* one of us?"

This time Hero responded. "You have had enough retribution, but we have not. You killed three of our kind, but we only killed two of your kind. You may now choose the one we must kill." Hero waited for Infinity's translator to fall silent then pointed his rifle at her head. "If you do not want to choose, I will choose for you."

Desmond stepped in front of Infinity. "Wait! This is crazy. We just agreed that we would exist together and help each other out. It makes no sense for you to want to kill another one of us!"

Hero continued aiming his rifle as he listened to the translation. Then he spoke. "You killed three of our kind as retribution for the actions of our genetic ancestors. We kill three of you as retribution for the actions you yourselves took. Perhaps you should reconsider what makes sense and what does not make sense."

Infinity stepped up to Desmond's side. Hero was less than ten yards out. She might be able to rush the bastard and disarm him, although that hadn't worked out so well the previous day. And with dozens of other armed Outlanders here, what would be the point? She considered this, then tensed her muscles, preparing to try it anyway. There *was* a point to it—if the Outlanders were going to kill one of them, it was going to be her, and she was going to die on her own terms.

"Don't do it, Infinity," Desmond hissed, apparently recognizing her intent. "Even if you manage to take one out, it'll just give them reason to kill yet another of us."

"Just stop your goddamn bickering!" Gibson said. "I swear, you people really are worse than the damn monkey-frogs."

Infinity swung around. Gibson was still sitting on the ground, and he had pulled off his crude tourniquet. Blood was pouring out into a growing puddle in the grass.

Vic rushed over and snatched up the t-shirt. "What the hell, man? Put this back on."

Gibson flailed his good arm, pushing Vic aside. "Back off!" He then leveled his gaze at Infinity, and she could see that he was fading fast. His face was pale, and one eyelid was drooping, almost shut. "A life for a life," he said. "It's what they want. Don't be stupid... you're not gonna talk 'em out of it."

Gibson's four mates were now at his side, begging him to stop. Tessa grabbed the t-shirt from Vic and attempted to wrap it around Gibson's arm.

He shook her off. "Jesus Christ, give me some dignity!"

The four women fell silent, unwilling to disobey him, even now.

Gibson rested his wrist on his knee with his severed hand dangling over the side and looked up at Hero. The wildcard's face was even paler than just moments before. "We've chosen. I'm the one. You're going to kill me." The translator on his other wrist promptly interpreted his words.

In the silence that followed the translation, Infinity could hear Gibson's blood dripping onto the grass.

Still at his full height, Hero strode forward. He stopped before Gibson, then slowly folded his knees until his head was only slightly higher than the wildcard's. Gibson held the Outlander's gaze for a moment, but soon his head rolled forward until it was resting on his arm and knee.

Hero swiveled his head, his four eyes appraising the other migrants. His shoulder limbs unfolded, and the finger-like tips wiped his lower pair of eyes then his upper pair before folding back up. He spoke, and Gibson's translator said, "This being appears to be dying."

"He wants you to kill him," Infinity said. "You told us to choose, and he chose himself."

Hero turned back to Gibson. He extended one of his arms and held a long finger under the diminishing flow of blood from the wildcard's wrist. The Outlander lifted the finger to his eyes and studied the blood.

"He wants you to kill him!" Infinity repeated. She was beginning to worry that if Gibson died on his own, the Outlanders might still feel the need to kill one more human.

Hero didn't reply. He simply remained in his crab-like crouch, staring at the bleeding man before him. Gibson's head rolled to the side, pulling his entire body with it. He collapsed onto the grass, his eyes half open and lifeless.

Hero gingerly lifted Gibson's hand, pulling the arm off the ground by the flap of skin. The flow of blood had stopped.

Infinity scanned the faces of Gibson's four mates. They were staring at his body without expression and without tears.

Hero turned away from Gibson and crab-walked back to his original position. Most of the other Outlanders were now folding their legs, lowering their bodies. They spoke to each other, a conversation ignored by the humans' translators. Hero went to Gideon and deftly untied the cord around the guardsman's neck. Next he freed Xavier, Richard, and Poppy.

The four humans massaged their throats as they cautiously stepped over to Infinity and the other migrants.

Bard spoke. Poppy's translator was now nearest, and it responded. "We have had enough retribution."

16

ABSOLUTION

MAY 3 - 5:31 PM

DESMOND GAZED at the three mounds of fresh soil, each about six feet long and two feet wide. He and the other migrants had been on this world less than thirty-six hours and had already buried three people. Fourteen percent of the colony. Fourteen percent of the humans existing on this version of Earth.

He kneeled and put a hand on the dirt piled on top of Emily's grave. He closed his eyes and projected several visual memories from his mind, through his arm, and into the soil. They were memories of better times on the arthropod world. He recalled Emily smiling and laughing, her face lit by a dried-moss fire in the center chamber of Mossview, the colony's shelter. He thought of the time he had strolled around the edge of a framework hill and had discovered Emily and Steven in an embarrassingly passionate embrace. Finally, he thought of the time she had overcooked the meat from a thirty-pound hermit crab. She had apologized to the others so profusely that everyone finally decided to eat the meat anyway, just to appease her guilt.

Desmond figured his projected thoughts had simply dissipated into the soil, and even if they somehow got through, Emily was now nothing more than dead cells. He projected the thoughts anyway, just in case. Then he moved to Steven's grave and did the same.

When he got to Gibson's grave, he paused, contemplating. The man had displayed unpredictable behaviors and uncertain qualities —definitely a wildcard. Unfortunately, his best qualities would be acknowledged only in hindsight.

Desmond pressed his palm to the mound of soil and projected mental words. "Perhaps I owe you more than one thought, but I'll simply say I'm pretty sure someone else would now be buried in this spot if you hadn't... well, volunteered. I'll make sure people remember that."

Desmond stood and turned to the others. Instead of speaking words aloud, everyone had agreed to silently express whatever they felt was appropriate. Apparently, Desmond was the last to finish.

The Outlanders were waiting patiently at the edge of the field. Although they seemed baffled by the humans' desire to bury their dead, they had eagerly volunteered to dig the three holes. The task had taken them only a few minutes, even though they'd used nothing more than hand-sized tools they had pulled from their waist packs. Desmond was starting to appreciate the benefits of having eight extremities capable of manipulating tools.

He and the other migrants left the forest to join the Outlanders.

Infinity spoke to the beings. "We would be willing to help you carry your dead companions back to your city."

"Our dead companions are dead," Bard replied. "Why would we want them in our city?"

Infinity obviously struggled to come up with an answer, which almost made Desmond smile in spite of the circumstances. "Well, never mind then," she finally said.

"I guess I'll be the one to ask the obvious question," Lenny said. He was still holding a hand over the knife wound on his shoulder, even though Poppy had already cleaned and stitched it. "What the hell is next?"

Desmond tilted his head toward the Outlanders. "You should probably ask them."

Lenny made a *well, duh* face and turned to Bard. "I think we'll eventually have a slew of questions for you guys. I suppose most of them can wait, though. You should realize it'll take some serious time before some of us can figure out how to get comfortable talking to you. I mean, seriously, you've killed our people and we've killed yours. Not what I'd call a great icebreaker. I guess what I want to ask is, what the hell should we be doing next?"

Lenny's translator began buzzing and clicking.

Xavier nudged Lenny's elbow. "You really think they're going to understand any of what you just said? Are you even aware you're talking through a language translator?"

The buzzing and clicking ended. Bard spoke, and Lenny's translator said, "We understand. Perhaps for now you wish to return to the site where we first found you, your camp. We will take you to your camp so that you do not have to walk there after the day's light is diminished."

After the translation ended, Lenny smirked at Xavier.

Fisher pumped his arms to speak, and this time Donica's translator interpreted. "When you figure out how to get comfortable talking to us, we will get to know you better, and you will get to know us better. We have questions to ask you, and we have stories to tell you. We have a production factory, given to us by our creators, the black-fur beings. We will show you how to use our production factory."

Another Outlander, one Desmond didn't recognize, moved closer. "You will use our factory to produce the parts you need to build your own city. We will observe how you design and construct your city. Perhaps your city will give us new ideas for how we can improve our city."

After the translation, another new Outlander spoke. "We will also observe how your species produces offspring. We have learned about the reproduction of offspring in some of the animals that live on this island and in the sea, and you are similar to those animals, but you are also different from those animals. We will be pleased to observe."

Bard spoke up again. "We will be pleased to learn much from you, and as we learn, and as we learn more, and as we learn more after that, we will someday build a great city. And you will build a great city. We will someday build a second city, and you will build a second city. Someday we will have a civilization as great as our genetic ancestors. The black-fur beings will return to this world, and they will be pleased with our civilization. The black-fur beings created us, and therefore we will be pleased to make them proud of our civilization."

After listening to the translation of Bard's spiel, Lenny gave Desmond an exasperated look. "I just wanted to know what we do next. As in right now, not in the next thousand years."

Desmond was starting to realize Kitty had been serious when she had told him these beings would only reach their full potential in the presence of another sentient species. The Outlanders were obviously highly skilled and intelligent, but their thought sequences tended to run completely off the tracks. Perhaps their genetic ancestors had some kind of mutualistic relationship with a species capable of reining them in.

Desmond stepped closer to Infinity and took her hand in his. Surprisingly, she didn't pull away. Then he spoke to the Outlanders. "We're on board with all of this. It *is* better than killing each other. I'm going to be honest with you, though. The main reason we are willing to begin this partnership is we intend to prevent your species from ever doing what your genetic ancestors did. That's how we'll find absolution for the things we've done to our own world and to other worlds. We will make sure that our offspring carry on this effort after we die, and we'll make sure they teach their offspring to do the same, and their offspring after that. You need to know this—as long as our species exists on this world, we will become your enemy if you ever start assuming it's your job to destroy other civilizations. And we will expect you to do the same for us."

The Outlanders spoke to each other for a minute or so. Then Bard returned his attention to the humans. The being spoke briefly, and Desmond's translator simply said, "We are pleased."

17

———

CITY

MAY 3 - 6:15 PM

INFINITY STRUGGLED to process the head-spinning series of events of the last two days, particularly the last few hours. The Outlanders were now leading her and the other migrants across the vast field toward the city. She had come here to kill these bastards, and now she was supposed to consider them friends and neighbors. Understanding why was one thing, being able to achieve it was another. It was going to take time.

She would also need time to sort out what happened between her and Desmond. The hollowness inside her was not as intense now, but it was still there. Maybe it was irrational, but she couldn't shake the feeling he had suddenly figured out she wasn't the kind of person he could love. Infinity had never really believed she was the kind of person *anybody* could love, and now Desmond had discovered this to be true.

Desmond had been walking in front of her, but now he slowed until she was at his side, and he took her hand. She considered refusing but decided his hand felt comforting. "If you're thinking of pushing thoughts into my head, don't," she said. "I'm not in the mood." She glanced at him. He looked like he'd just lost an MMA cage fight, but then so did most of the other migrants. At least they were alive.

"Have I told you you're brilliant?" he asked.

She decided not to answer. She wasn't in the mood for stupid small talk either.

He sighed loudly. "Here's the way I'm going to look at this situation. What happened today? It was our first fight as a couple. Every couple has to have a first fight. It's like we're married now." He tilted his head back and put a hand to his throat. "I feel like I have a bruise on my neck. Do I have a bruise on my neck?"

"I didn't take you down that hard."

"Really? Because I may have a bruise on my back too."

She gave in and released a brief snort. "This wasn't our first fight. When we have our first fight, you'll know it."

They walked in silence for a few seconds.

Desmond said, "I noticed you chose not to tell the Outlanders about Kitty bridging to this world. Surprised me a bit."

"Telling them might have helped convince them. Maybe. I decided I didn't want them to know Kitty threatened us, though. I'd rather the Outlanders believe Kitty's people have respect for us humans."

"If the black-fur beings respect us, the Outlanders will respect us," he said.

"Exactly."

They went back to walking in silence.

The Outlanders led them into the gap at the north end of the field. The gap turned out to be a well-worn path, several hundred yards long with dense forest on either side. The far end of the corridor opened onto the beach. Rising from the beach and out into the sea was the framework structure of the city.

The beach and water beneath the city were both surprisingly clean. In fact, other than two submarines lashed to the supports at the offshore end of the city, there was nothing at all other than Outlander footprints in the sand—no other vehicles, no unused construction materials, not even any trash. In fact, Infinity didn't even see a way to get up to the city itself. The pale tan support columns were all smooth, without ladder rungs or stairs.

This mystery was solved by the time the group came to a stop beneath the onshore edge of the framework. Three bowl-shaped containers, each about ten feet across and suspended by three cables, began descending from the lowest arrangement of cross girders and walkways, which was at least thirty feet above the beach. The bowls came to rest on the sand.

Bard spoke to the humans. "We must move through the lower level of our city to take you to our... *water vehicles*. Today you have killed three of our kind, so this is not the appropriate time to show you the other levels of our city. Some of our younger offspring may feel a greater need for retribution than we feel as mature adults. If they kill more of you, then you would have to kill more of us."

"Oh, yeah," Lenny said. "I say we avoid the little whipper-snappers."

Bard crawled smoothly into one of the bowls, his toes gripping the edges and his long legs easily bracing the bowl to prevent it from tipping. Hero got in beside him, then the two beings stared at the humans, apparently waiting for some of them to get in. Infinity shrugged and stepped forward. The four remaining wildcards joined her at the bowl's lip, and they all awkwardly crawled in. If Bard and Hero hadn't stabilized the container, Infinity was pretty sure she and the other women would have flopped the bowl onto its side. Now they were sliding around on the bowl's smooth interior surface, trying to find firm footing without falling on their butts. The Outlanders' bare feet, however, seemed to be gripping the surface securely.

As several Outlanders and the other humans began piling into the two remaining containers, Infinity's bowl began rising. The motion caused her feet to slip, and she almost tumbled to the floor. Latonya actually *did* fall, knocking Tessa on top of her in the process.

The bowl came to a stop with its lip at floor level. Infinity scrambled out first, glad to be rid of the damn thing. The lift may have suited the Outlanders' strange bodies, but it sucked for humans. This was when she saw how the elevators actually worked. Another Outlander was crouched within a covered booth to the side. The being was turning two small wheels, one with his foot and the other with one hand. His other hand was resting upon a third wheel without turning it, presumably the wheel that controlled Infinity's lift. There were no motors behind the wheels, only an impressive set of interlocking gears. The Outlander was manually lifting bowls containing at least a thousand pounds each, and doing it with no apparent effort.

Everything she could see in this place was either black or pale tan and appeared to be made of the same smooth, plastic-like substance.

Infinity turned to Bard. "Does all this stuff come from the factory the black-fur beings left for you?"

Bard listened to the translation then pointed through the city's framework to the distant structure about a mile out to sea that Infinity had spotted earlier from the beach. "You are correct. Our production factory allows us to make the parts we need."

Desmond had crawled out of his bowl lift and was now beside Infinity. "Do you people not have electricity? Or motors? All I see here are mechanical devices."

Bard listened to the translation and hesitated before answering. "Your translating device has failed to make your words entirely clear to me. Perhaps the concepts you are asking about are things we can learn from you. We would be pleased to learn about such things if they will help us improve our city."

"They don't have electricity?" Xavier exclaimed as he stepped up between Infinity and Desmond. "Their ancestors invented bridging technology. How can they not even have electricity?"

Bard spoke, and Infinity's translator said, "Our production factory allows us to produce objects of any size or shape. We use the objects to construct our city, our tools, and everything else we need. We enjoy learning how to fit these objects together in such ways as to perform many tasks. Our water vehicles are our greatest achievement, and we will be pleased to show them to you now. We will take you to your camp in one of our water vehicles."

Another of the Outlanders added, "We would like for you to examine our city and our water vehicles. With your wisdom, you will certainly have suggestions for us to improve them."

Hero then said, "You will have suggestions for us, but your bodies are so different from ours. Your legs are short, and you have no tails. If we follow your suggestions, we will make new water vehicles that are no longer appropriate for our bodies. We will hardly fit within them."

Another Outlander joined this bizarre line of reasoning. "Our city will then have dwellings that are suitable only to your bodies, and we will feel much discomfort."

Infinity turned to Desmond. "They're doing it again."

Yet another of the beings said, "Our offspring will grow in size, but they will not understand why their dwellings and their tools do not fit their bodies and hands. They will wonder why we have imposed so many discomforts upon them, and they will begin to question us as their teachers."

Hero said, "Our offspring will then decide they can build a better city and better tools, and they will leave us to begin their own city. They will leave before we have taught them all they need to know."

Infinity turned to Desmond again. "You're the one who likes talking to them. You deal with this." She left his side and made her way along a walkway to the west edge of the framework. Fortunately, none of the Outlanders followed her. Standing so near them was starting to fray her nerves. She stood alone thirty feet above the beach on a walkway that had no safety railing and gazed out over the water. The sun was already low in the west, although it wouldn't set for over an hour. Gentle waves and ripples on the sea created a stippled, sparkling reflection. In the center of the reflection, four glistening backs broke the surface momentarily and glided back under. Then at least a dozen more emerged just behind those. The creatures were about the size of dolphins but without dorsal fins. They cut through the water gracefully, apparently not in a hurry to get anywhere.

Infinity had long ago lost track of all the different versions of Earth she had bridged to, and she had grown to love the arthropod world, but none of those places were as beautiful as this. Something about the islands and the water, as well as the nearly perfect climate, soothed the turmoil she felt regarding the Outlanders.

Would she ever feel safe sharing this island with these beings? Such an existence was hard to imagine, but now she could at least admit to herself that it might be possible. She also wanted a life with Desmond, although she was uncertain their relationship could ever be the same after what happened today.

Infinity scanned the handful of other islands she could see from where she was standing. Did a similar arrangement of small islands go on forever on this world? Or was there a massive continent just over the horizon, or perhaps thousands of miles from here? Regardless, all the islands she could see were supposedly uninhabited by sentient beings, although they were probably home to countless creatures no human had ever seen before. Infinity couldn't get overly excited about those creatures, as long as they weren't a threat to her colony, but Desmond would. He'd probably be thrilled to spend the rest of his life exploring this place and giving stupid names to all the lifeforms.

These thoughts of Desmond actually gave her a slight urge to smile. On several occasions yesterday she had enjoyed smiling, but now she was hesitant to let down her guard.

Infinity heard something shuffling above her. She stepped as close as she dared to the walkway's edge and craned her neck to look up at the framework and pill-shaped dwellings. An Outlander was staring back at her from about forty feet above where she stood. It took her a moment to realize the being was hanging upside down, with his two-pronged tail wrapped around one of the supports. His spindly legs dangled outward at odd angles. He remained motionless, watching her with two pairs of eyes. This Outlander was smaller than the others she'd seen, perhaps only half the size.

"Infinity," Desmond called from behind her. "You coming?"

She turned back to him and nodded. Then she returned her gaze to the juvenile Outlander above, who was still staring down at her. After letting out a sigh, she raised a hand and waved. It was an idiotic thing to do—the gesture wouldn't mean anything to an alien being.

The kid straightened one of his legs a bit and waved back with his foot, curling and then extending all three toes.

Apparently, the only way to get down to the two whale-subs floating beside the city's supports was to climb down a pathetic excuse for a ladder. Infinity watched Hero and Bard as they easily scrambled down. The ladder, which looked more like an oversized coiled spring, was made for beings with seven-foot legs. The coils were at least four feet apart.

Fisher and a half dozen other Outlanders stood in their crab stance to the side, waiting for the humans to climb down next.

"My turn," Lenny said. "I wanna be the first human to ever touch an alien submarine."

Infinity pointed to the nearest side of the coiled spring. "Stay on this side. If you fall, you'll hit the water, not the sub."

Lenny lightly patted the stitched knife wound on his shoulder and said, "Words of wisdom." He got to his knees and carefully lowered himself onto the coil.

One at a time, the others started down after him.

While waiting to go down, Desmond turned to Infinity and held out a hand, palm up. "Why don't you let me use that walkie talkie. I'll let the others know we're coming back."

She pulled it from her pocket. "I'll do it." She turned it on and pressed the talk button. "Armando, are you there?"

Several seconds later, the device clicked and Armando's voice came through the tiny speaker. "I'm here, Infinity. I've been waiting anxiously to hear from you. Are you okay?"

"Yes, most of us are fine. A lot has happened. We'll explain everything when we get back to camp. Armando, you and the others might want to go down to the beach in the next few minutes. We'll meet you there soon, okay?"

There was a pause of several seconds. "Okay."

"Good, then we'll see you soon." She switched off the device and put it away to avoid explaining further.

Surprisingly, everyone made it to the submarine's deck without taking an involuntary swim. The vessel was at least fifteen feet wide here in the center, although it was tapered toward the nose and tail. Other than a flat portion of its back, on which the humans and Outlanders stood, the machine was shaped like a huge ocean creature. Or at least one with a body made of jointed segments. Infinity could see fins protruding on either side just below the surface.

"Look at that," Desmond said, pointing to the machine's tail. "Instead of horizontal flukes like a whale, this thing's tail is long and vertical, like a mudpuppy's. This isn't a whale-sub, it's a salamander-sub."

"Call it what you want," Infinity said. "I just want it to be safe."

Xavier was standing with his feet spread wide to counteract the sub's gentle rocking. "It doesn't feel terribly safe to me."

"Well, we're about to find out," Lenny said. "Truth be told, the uncertainty of it gives me a warm, fuzzy pucker. Let's do this."

Bard was standing beside a round hatch at the rear of the flattened area. He pumped his arms to speak. "We wish for you to enter our water vehicle. There will be room for all of you inside."

Lenny rushed forward to be first.

When it was Infinity's turn, she found a smaller version of the coiled spring inside the hatch, which was much easier to navigate. Once inside, she realized the sub's egg-shaped interior was actually deeper than it was wide, perhaps because of the Outlanders' fondness for vertical spaces. As Bard had said, there was room for all twelve of the humans, as well as six Outlanders. But it was crowded, and the sub's interior had an unidentifiable and unpleasant odor, reminding Infinity of the smell of fish guts.

There appeared to be only one room in the sub for passengers and crew, and the space was surprisingly bare and simple. Instead of instrument panels with digital screens and buttons, there were only a few small wheels to turn, similar to those the Outlanders used to raise the bowl-shaped elevators. Four wheels were mounted on the back wall, presumably to control the sub's tail, and two were affixed to each side wall, maybe to control the fins. That was it—nothing but mechanical controls. Infinity envisioned complex interlocking gears behind the walls that made it possible for the Outlanders to power the sub with no more than the muscles of their arms and legs.

Most impressive—in fact, almost breathtaking—was the view out the front of the sub. At the nose end the smooth interior walls gave way to a series of curved, vertical windows. These windows were in the same shape as the machine's segments that could be seen from outside the sub. Those jointed segments were probably what allowed the submarine to move like a sea creature. Here at the front, though, the segments were transparent. The top half of each window was above the surface, providing a view of the waves, the beach, and the forest beyond. The bottom half provided a view of a completely different world below.

Infinity pushed her way past some of the other migrants to get closer to the sub's nose. The windows of the nose were arranged in the shape of a cone, allowing views to the sides as well as up and down. The water appeared to be about twenty feet deep here, and Infinity saw schools of hundreds of small fish—or maybe amphibians—darting back and forth, changing direction for no apparent reason. Several larger creatures swam slowly along the bottom, stirring up clouds as they rooted through the sand for whatever the hell they were looking for.

She gazed out toward deeper water. Some distance out, on the edge of visibility, three massive shapes were swimming slowly from east to west. Although she couldn't see details, each of the creatures had to be at least twenty feet long.

"Maybe I've died and gone to heaven," Desmond said. He had snuck up beside her and was gazing downward at the underwater view.

"Thought you might like this," she said quietly.

The sub shifted to the left. Infinity staggered and had to embrace Desmond to stay on her feet. Then the sub shifted to the right, and back to the left. It continued shifting, and she realized the sub was now swimming forward. She planted her feet securely and turned to the rear of the cabin. Two Outlanders were against the back wall, each bracing himself in place with one foot on the floor and the other gripping a handle about eight feet up the wall that seemed to be there for this very purpose. Each Outlander was using his shorter arms to crank two of the control wheels mounted on the back wall. The entire sub continued shifting side to side as the tail propelled it forward, but the shifts were becoming less extreme. As the sub picked up speed, the side-to-side motion diminished until Infinity and Desmond could release each other and stand without much wobbling.

Two more Outlanders had stationed themselves at the wheels on the side walls, gazing over the humans' heads out the front viewing windows. Occasionally they would crank the wheels one way and then the other, apparently steering the sub by moving its side fins.

Infinity scanned the other migrants' faces. Most of them were staring straight ahead while awkwardly tipping to the left and right. Everyone had to stand because the cabin was without seats. Random handles of various lengths and shapes extended from the walls, but these were obviously designed for the Outlanders, and many were higher than humans could reach.

The sub swam out into deeper water, still only half submerged. Infinity gazed at the sheer cliff face to the east of the city as the Outlanders steered the sub out and around the dangerous rocks. Abruptly, her view of the cliffs disappeared as the sub dove under. Out here the sea looked to be about thirty feet deep, but the Outlanders kept the sub just under the surface. Perhaps the machine wasn't designed to go any deeper.

"I have a theory," Desmond said.

Infinity glanced at him. "Of course you do."

He ignored this. "These Outlanders are intelligent. Probably more intelligent than we are. But their civilization here is young. Kitty's people created them from genetic instructions, but clones don't have any knowledge or memories from the originals, right?"

Infinity didn't bother to answer.

"So, these Outlanders are starting from scratch. All they know is what Kitty's people have taught them. Plus, they have a factory that can apparently produce just about any type of solid object you could want, maybe like a 3D printer on steroids."

Infinity gave an impatient nod. "And?"

"These Outlanders can create any machine they can think of, as long as the machine is composed only of solid objects made of the exact same material—maybe some kind of composite plastic stuff generated from elements in sea water. This may explain why the factory was placed offshore."

"Makes sense so far," she said, but she was turning her attention to the view outside. The sub was now swimming through a sea of plants, attached to the sandy bottom below and growing up almost to the water's surface. She could hear the plants softly brushing against the viewing windows as they passed by.

Desmond went on. "I don't know why Kitty's people didn't leave the Outlanders more than one factory. They could have left a chemical or pharmaceutical plant. They could have left a facility for generating electricity, along with a factory for making electrical components. They could have—"

"I get it," she said, turning back to him. "Maybe Kitty's people plan to provide those things later. Or maybe they just wanted to give the Outlanders a kickstart and see what happens next. Does it really matter?"

He twisted his mouth to the side for a moment. "Well, my theory is about this submarine. The Outlanders obviously love the water. They decided they wanted a vehicle to help them get around in the sea. So, they designed one based on the only large things they were familiar with that could move efficiently through the water— whale-salamanders, like the big fat egg-layers we saw yesterday."

Infinity decided to add to this, otherwise it could go on forever. "And because they don't have electricity, motors, or any of that crap, they made the whole submarine as a simple mechanical machine."

"Precisely," he said. Then he gave her a smug look, obviously considering his theory to be brilliant. Actually, it was, but she wasn't tempted to admit it.

She gazed at his face. Then she furrowed her brows. "Do you realize your nose is broken?" She reached for it. "Hold steady a second. I'll just—"

He pulled back. "No! No thank you. I'll just... have Poppy look at it later."

Infinity felt the corners of her mouth starting to lift slightly, and she turned back to the viewing windows. The sub was now surfacing. The water level rippled down the windows until the top half of the viewing area was once again exposed to the air. The floating sub was now swimming straight for the beach. There was Armando, standing at the edge of the surf and staring out at the submarine. He was flanked by the other migrants who had remained at the camp.

The Outlanders brought the sub to a stop just as its nose nudged up against a wide cluster of corals. Without speaking, Bard clambered up to the hatch, opened it, and crawled out. He then stuck his head back through and stared at the humans, apparently waiting for them.

Once again, Lenny rushed forward to be first.

When Infinity crawled onto the deck and got to her feet, Lenny was waving toward shore while Isabelle was helping Daisy wave her tiny hand back at him. The sub was still at least a hundred yards from the beach, and Infinity saw no way to get across the expanse of water, other than swimming. Maybe her group should have turned down the submarine ride and walked back to camp.

When the last migrant had emerged onto the deck, Bard spoke. Infinity's translator said, "We are pleased that you have observed our water vehicle. When you construct your own water vehicles, we will observe them. Such observations will give us ideas for improving our own water vehicles. We will learn from you, and you will learn from us. We will come to your camp again soon. You should talk to the others at your camp. Explain to them that you have had enough retribution, and we will explain to our offspring that we have had enough retribution. Then there will be no more killing. Now we will return to our city before the day's light becomes diminished."

Hero and Fisher had also emerged from the sub, and the three Outlanders stood silently as if waiting.

Now Infinity was really concerned. "Um, is there any way we can get from here to the beach without swimming? In case you forgot, yesterday we were attacked by predators in the water."

After the translation, Bard stepped over to the hatch and spoke down to the Outlanders who had stayed inside. Seconds later, three rifles were shoved through the hatch from below. Bard handed one each to Fisher and Hero and kept the third. He then turned his gaze to Infinity and moved his arms to speak. Her translator said, "Soon you will learn your own methods of avoiding the predators of the sea, and we will be pleased to observe your methods. Perhaps we will learn better methods from observing. For now, we will help you avoid the predators. You should observe and learn."

Just as the translation ended, Bard, Hero, and Fisher launched themselves from the deck. Infinity watched them glide beneath the water's surface for about twenty yards before their heads emerged. The three beings bobbed silently, probably because their sound-producing armpits were now under water.

"If there's anyone here who doesn't know how to swim, you'd better speak up now," Infinity said to the migrants.

"I know how," said Xavier, "but I'd rather not."

Desmond stepped up to the edge. "Bard said he'll protect us, and I believe him. You should too." Then he jumped feet-first into the sea. His head popped up and he said, "Last one to the beach has to explain to the others everything that happened today."

This seemed to work. The migrants threw themselves into the water and started swimming.

Infinity waited until they were all in the water then watched the three Outlanders. The beings had gone under, and she could see their dark shapes swimming back and forth alongside the less graceful humans, supposedly protecting them. Satisfied, she dove in and swam slowly behind the other migrants. She'd be the last to arrive at the beach, but that was okay—she wanted to be the one to tell the story to Armando anyway.

18
____

MUTUALISM

Nine Days Later - May 12

AFTER ASKING NO FEWER than four people where Armando was, Desmond finally found his former boss on the beach scribbling something in his notebook. Towering above Armando were several stacks of construction tubes and connectors, intended for the eventual framework for the human city. The Outlanders still frequently proclaimed that they would be pleased to observe how the migrants designed a city, but they couldn't seem to resist providing an ever-growing collection of building components. Not to mention a seemingly endless stream of suggestions for how they could be used.

Armando glanced up and smiled warmly as Desmond approached. "You will not be surprised, Desmond, to hear I have changed my mind yet again. In spite of encouragement from the Outlanders to construct our city over the water as they have done, I'm going to recommend building on the hillside. I believe we must embrace our own history and biological heritage—we are not semi-aquatic creatures, as the Outlanders seem to be. Nor are we fond of climbing to death-defying heights as a matter of daily routine." He held out his notebook for Desmond to see. "Therefore, I will propose to our people this design, or something thereabouts."

Desmond shaded his eyes and studied the sketch. "What am I looking at?"

Armando pointed with his pen. "The framework will be upon the hillside rather than over the beach or the water. It will have clear views of the sea, of course—Infinity wouldn't have it otherwise—but our dwellings will be low, just above the treetops. I honestly don't see us becoming accustomed to spherical or pill-shaped enclosures. Instead, our dwellings will be based upon various configurations of rectangular modules." He gestured toward the massive piles of tubes and connectors. "We can request any components we wish, and we can fit them together any way we wish. Honestly, we're limited only by our imaginations."

Desmond eyed the stacks. All the pieces were the same color—light tan. Despite their monstrous size and uniform color, the pieces reminded him of several building sets he'd owned as a young child. The components delivered by the Outlanders were generic pieces of various lengths and thicknesses, but they literally could be snapped together in any arrangement. The possible configurations were endless, and the material, although strong, was lightweight. The migrants would be able to carry even the largest pieces through the swamp and up the hillside.

"It sounds terrific," he said to Armando. "I'm sure the others will approve."

Armando smiled again, obviously pleased with himself. His eyes lingered on Desmond. "I sense that you have come to me with something else on your mind?"

Desmond glanced around the beach. None of the other migrants were around. "Well, yeah. I've been thinking. The day I went after Infinity's group to stop them from killing Outlanders—you talked to Kitty that day."

Armando furrowed his brows slightly. "And?"

"Do you think Kitty is going to come back?"

Armando looked down at the sand. "She didn't say. I doubt it."

"You didn't actually talk to Kitty that day, did you?"

The older man looked up, and his eyes widened momentarily. He studied Desmond's face. Finally, he said, "Does Infinity know?"

Desmond shook his head. "Probably not. *I* wasn't even sure until this moment. You just confirmed it. Actually, now that I think about it, I suspect you never really agreed with her about attacking the Outlanders in the first place."

Armando sighed and looked out over the surf. "No, I didn't." He turned back to Desmond. "I could see that she wanted me to, though. Perhaps she *needed* me to."

Desmond almost grimaced from a sudden pang of guilt. Armando had understood what Infinity needed at the time and had acted accordingly.

Armando went on. "I needed time to develop a plan, and when Infinity was ready to leave camp for the Outlander city, all I had come up with was the visit from Kitty. I needed something so decisive, so horrifying, that Infinity would have no choice but to suspend all attempts at violence. So, I gave her the walkie talkie. I theorized the only way to make a visit from Kitty seem believable would be to say Kitty visited while Infinity was away from camp. For it to be believable to those who had remained in camp with me, Kitty needed to visit me while I was off on my own." He shook his head. "In hindsight, it doesn't seem all that believable at all."

Desmond forced a smile. "No, it doesn't. Are you going to tell her?"

He shook his head again. "I do not know if I should. Are *you* going to tell her?"

"Not if I know what's good for me. You'll have to do it yourself. Or perhaps she'll figure it out." Desmond gazed at the older man, who was again staring at the sea. "Armando, you're a good person.

For my sake and for Infinity's, I'm thankful you bridged to this world with us."

Armando smiled slightly but continued gazing out over the water.

"You're a hard man to find, Des." It was Latonya's voice.

Desmond turned toward the forest to see all four of the remaining wildcards approaching, their legs wet to the knees with dirty swamp water.

Tessa said, "The first thing we need to do with those oversized Tinkertoys is build a walkway over the damn swamp."

"It's on the list," Armando said, turning away from the surf.

The four women stopped and stood shoulder to shoulder, all of them staring at Desmond.

He frowned. "What?"

"We've had a long discussion this morning," said Tessa. "And, well...."

"Just tell him!" Donica demanded.

Tessa took a deep breath. "Gibson is dead, and you're the one who killed him."

Desmond blinked. This was the last thing he'd expected. "You were there. You know I had no choice. I didn't—"

"Which means we're now *your* mates," Tessa stated matter-of-factly.

He gaped at them, completely at a loss for words.

"Good lord in heaven," Armando muttered.

"By the rules of our guild," said Sue, "we are now sworn to you. We will obey you, fight by your side, and bear your children. We will also....." Sue abruptly covered her mouth with her hand. "Dammit!" Her voice was now muffled. "I thought I could get through it, but I can't."

Tessa punched Sue's shoulder. "I knew I should have done it myself!"

All four of the wildcards were now grinning.

"Still worth it, though," Latonya exclaimed. "That look on your face, Des. Damn!"

Desmond realized his mouth was hanging open, and he shut it. "Seriously? You think that was funny?"

"Oh, it was funny alright," Latonya said.

Armando clapped his hands together twice. "Kudos to the wildcards. Ever unpredictable."

AGAIN, Desmond had to ask around, this time to find Infinity. Richard mentioned that she'd said something about going to the *fat-chin* camp. This was the name Lenny had given to the beings who had been slaughtered by the Outlanders. Infinity seemed fascinated by the demolished camp and had visited it almost daily.

Desmond made the half-mile walk, which was now easier due to a path that was becoming well worn, and found Infinity sitting cross-legged beside one of the shredded, decaying tents.

He sat on the ground beside her. She had arranged two of the fat-chin skulls on the ground, with the empty eye sockets staring back at her. One of the skulls was only half the size of the other.

She nodded toward the smaller skull. "I found this one a few days ago. They brought children with them."

Desmond picked up the skull, which was missing its lower jaw. Like the adult skulls, its teeth were pointed. A small, blue stone had been mounted firmly on the front of each tooth. Although these beings weren't exactly human, Desmond estimated this child to have been five or six years old. He said, "I guess we should consider ourselves lucky."

"Yeah."

"Is this why you come here? To look at these skulls?"

She shrugged. "I just wish I knew more about these people and what happened to them."

He put the skull back and gazed at her profile. "You and I don't talk about this much, but the other day Celia said something about how we might be the next ones to have a child. She may be right, you know."

She picked up the diminutive skull and placed it in the exact position it had been before Desmond had moved it. "That thought kind of scares me. It should scare you too. Besides, I'm not certain anything Kitty told us was actually true. Who knows if she really did fix my... you know, my system. It'd probably be best if she didn't."

Desmond put a hand on her knee, palm up. "She did or she didn't. Either way, you and I are okay, right? You and I together, I mean."

She put her hand in his. "Yeah, I want us to be." Then she gave his hand a hard squeeze. "Besides, there aren't too many others to choose from."

He squeezed back. "Um, speaking of that. I had a visit from the wildcards. All four of them."

She turned to him with one raised brow.

"Because I'm responsible for Gibson's death, they now want to be my mates. You don't mind sharing me, do you?"

She remained expressionless. "Why would I mind?"

"Oh, crap," Desmond said. "You knew! Did you put them up to that?"

"I may have mentioned the look on your face would make the effort worthwhile."

All at once Desmond felt as if a vise that was squeezing his brain had been removed. He chuckled. Then he laughed out loud, enough to make Infinity stare. He got it under control. "Sorry. That's really not funny, but it is."

They sat together without speaking for a few minutes, listening to two groups of monkey-frogs crowing furiously at each other in the distance, probably over something meaningless.

Finally, Desmond said, "Will you come with me this afternoon? I've already talked Lenny and Xavier into coming." He was referring to his third planned excursion with Hero, Bard, and Fisher. During the other two outings they had taken him to nearby islands. Each island seemed to have its own endemic species of terrestrial creatures. It was like the islands were separated by hundreds or thousands of miles rather than only two or three miles.

She stared at the two skulls for a moment, perhaps thinking about the offer. "Not that I want to miss listening to hours of nerd talk, but I'm not ready yet. You know... the Outlanders."

"They want to be our friends. When *will* you be ready?"

She shot him a glance. "You really think that's something I can just choose?"

"Of course not. I just... I love discovering more of this world, but I'd like to share those adventures with you."

She seemed to hesitate, then she scooted in front of him and patted his knee, her way of telling him to unfold his legs to make room. He was more than willing to do so. She sat between his legs and leaned back against his chest. This was a position that had long ago become both comforting and symbolic to both of them, although Desmond would be hard-pressed to express exactly what it symbolized. At this moment it simply meant that everything was going to be okay.

Desmond, Lenny and Xavier waited at the end of the long pier. The structure, which several days ago had been constructed in only a few hours by the Outlanders, allowed the migrants access to the whale-subs without risking their lives swimming a hundred yards out from shore. The Outlanders had seemed baffled by the humans' request for the pier, but, as always, they'd taken on the task with enthusiasm and uncanny skill.

Desmond had been most interested to see how the Outlanders would embed the pier's support pillars in the sand below the surf. Astoundingly, they had simply pulled a few handheld tools from their waist pouches and started excavating, demonstrating they could remain underwater far longer than humans could. In this way they had managed to get all sixteen pillars inserted about six feet into the substrate in record time. Once these supports were in place, they had snapped all the girders and decking together within minutes.

From watching the pier's construction, Desmond realized building the framework for the human city was going to be much easier than he'd imagined—assuming the Outlanders were willing to help embed the support pillars.

The whale-sub arrived just after noon, as promised. Hero, Bard, Fisher, and several other Outlanders emerged and immediately set to work. They had taken this opportunity to deliver yet another load of giant Tinkertoys. The Outlanders hoisted the pieces up through the sub's hatch. Then, one at a time, they tossed them into the water, dove in, and swam to shore dragging the pieces with them. The material was lighter than water, making the pieces float, which facilitated the process.

"We now have a perfectly good pier," Xavier said, watching the Outlanders, "and they still insist on swimming."

Desmond considered offering to carry some of the pieces but decided it would actually slow the process down.

A few minutes later, the pieces were stacked on the beach, and the Outlanders were back on the submarine's deck. Desmond, Lenny, and Xavier cautiously stepped from the pier to the sub's wet surface. On more than one occasion they had learned their hiking shoes did not grip the surface as well as the Outlanders' bare feet apparently did.

Once they were all inside with the hatch sealed, the two Outlanders at the fin controls on either side of the cabin expertly turned the wheels in certain ways, maneuvering the sub backward from the pier and turning it away from the beach. Bard spoke to the humans, and Desmond's translator said, "Perhaps you would like to operate our water vehicle." Bard led them to the four control wheels on the rear wall. Then he stood there, waiting.

Lenny said, "I guess this is a learn-as-you-go experience." He grabbed the lower wheel on the left and started turning it clockwise. The entire cabin rocked slightly to the left.

Desmond stepped up to the lower wheel on the right and copied Lenny's approach. The wheel, no more than a foot in diameter, was surprisingly easy to turn. The sub rocked to the right and then again to the left. The vessel was actually starting to swim forward.

Xavier stepped up between Desmond and Lenny and tried reaching for one of the top wheels, but they were both too high. "I don't know what those wheels do," he said, "but maybe we should leave this to the experts before we crash this thing into a coral boulder."

Desmond and Lenny released their wheels and stepped back. "Thanks, but we're better suited for terrestrial vehicles," Lenny said to Bard. "You know, driving cars into ditches, running red lights—stuff like that."

"How can you think it's helpful to intentionally confuse them?" Xavier asked.

Lenny just shrugged as the two Outlanders Armando had named Sailor and Skipper quickly moved in and took over the control wheels, bracing themselves against the wall with their long legs.

Bard gestured for the humans to move to the new "seats" the Outlanders had recently installed. The seats weren't much more than flat platforms projecting from the curved wall, but at least they each had a bar on the side that could be gripped when the sub was shifting back and forth excessively.

When they were seated, Bard spoke. Lenny's translator said, "We know you are pleased to observe creatures that inhabit the islands of this world. Today we are taking you to an island we believe you will find particularly pleasing. This island is distant, so we now have some time to get to know each other better. You will ask us questions, and we will ask you questions."

Desmond exchanged glances with Lenny and Xavier.

"This is rather abrupt," Xavier said. "I need to think a moment,"

Lenny said, "The dog ate my homework. I got nothin'."

Desmond turned back to Bard. "Okay. Here's a question. How do you make those sounds with your arms when you speak?"

Immediately after the translation, Bard lifted one of his diminutive arms, revealing a tennis-ball-sized biological structure in the flesh of his armpit. It looked like thin, rigid bone or cartilage positioned over a hollow space. With his other hand, Bard tapped the structure with one finger, resulting in surprisingly loud clicks.

"Holy crap," Lenny said. "That's a tymbal, like cicadas have under their wings! Cicadas produce clicks and buzzes in their tymbals to communicate. Wicked cool!"

Bard lowered his arm and pumped it rapidly, producing the sounds of his language. Lenny's translator interpreted. "We find it strange that you and many of the creatures of this world speak from your mouths."

This initiated an extended discussion of language and verbal communication.

After Desmond had exhausted his limited knowledge on this topic, he was ready to ask another question. He spoke to Bard. "That day our people killed three of your species, you told us that you sensed those individuals had died. How can that be possible?"

Bard's shoulder extremities unfolded. They wiped the surfaces of his lower pair of eyes then the upper pair before folding back into his shoulders. He spoke, and Desmond's translator interpreted.

"Some things are simple and uncomplicated. However, those simple, uncomplicated things are sometimes the most difficult to explain. We sense each other's presence. We have always sensed each other's presence, and we do not consider why or how it can be possible. I do not need to search this water vehicle to know that there are six of my species with me here. I do not need to go back to my city to know there are fifty-two of my species there. Four of them are in the pasture with our frog-steeds. Three are in the water, probably attending to our revered aquatic livestock. Nine are young offspring, still learning from our caretakers the ways of our species and the ways of this world."

Bard paused to allow the translation to catch up before continuing. "If one of our young offspring were to be careless and fall from the highest level of our city and die, I would know that now there are only eight young offspring in our city." He paused again.

Desmond waited for more, but apparently this was the extent of the explanation. What Bard had described seemed impossible. Then again, Desmond himself had been given the ability to project his thoughts into the minds of others through physical touch. He was learning to adjust his opinion of what was possible and what was not.

The questions continued for at least half an hour. Desmond, Lenny, and Xavier asked what the Outlanders did for entertainment, about their livestock, and what they'd been told by their parents and grandparents about the black-fur beings. Bard and his companions asked questions about the great cities of the humans' destroyed version of Earth. Coming up with coherent answers wasn't easy, and Desmond suspected the Outlanders were becoming more confused with every passing minute.

The sub came to a jolting halt. Desmond turned to the viewing windows. The craft was now wedged against a gradually-rising sandy bottom dotted with seagrasses. The top half of the windows revealed a thin strip of beach no more than forty yards from the sub's nose. A dense forest loomed beyond the beach, and no tall hills were visible.

Bard spoke, and Desmond's translator said, "We believe you will be pleased to observe one particularly interesting species we have found upon this island. However, the creature only resides at the island's interior, beyond the dense forest near the beach. If you are not inclined to walk to the interior, we would be pleased to go to a different island."

Lenny rubbed his hands together. "Are you kidding? You had me at *particularly interesting species!*" For the last three words he did a dubious impression of the voice from Desmond's translator.

"We're all willing to walk to the interior," Desmond said to Bard.

The beach was only a short swim away, but the Outlanders took their rifles and swam on either side of the humans, providing protection. Once on dry land, the Outlanders wasted no time. Without discussion, they led the group into the forest.

Desmond quickly realized this forest was fundamentally different from what he'd seen on the other islands. Massive cypress-like trees, each surrounded by dozens of shoulder-high "knees," were abundant. Some of the cypress knees appeared to be splattered with a yellow, gooey substance. Upon closer inspection, Desmond realized the stuff resembled slime mold, also called myxomycetes, a bizarre fungus-like organism he'd seen occasionally on his home world. He'd never seen slime molds this extensive, though. Also, these things were fast. They were visibly moving before his eyes, their blob-like tentacles flowing over the cypress knees at perhaps an inch per minute.

"Un-freaking-believable," Lenny said. He was now beside Desmond, staring at the slime mold.

Bard, Hero, and Fisher had paused to wait for them, so Desmond nudged Lenny and they all moved on. Time after time, the Outlanders had to wait patiently as the three biologists stopped to ogle another creature or another plant—even a few wriggling things they had no idea how to classify. Desmond and his former college roommates were now truly in their element.

After they had trekked through the dense forest for roughly a mile, the landscape opened up into a wide savanna.

Desmond stared, suddenly questioning his sense of scale. The savanna was dotted with tall plants, but they weren't actually trees. The plants appeared to be some kind of agave, or maybe yucca. Numerous sword-like leaves protruded outward from a center stem at the ground level. An extremely straight and tall stalk emerged from the center of each cluster of spreading leaves.

This general structure wasn't unusual—Desmond had seen plenty of similar plants back on his own version of Earth. What was surprising was the scale. The spreading clusters of leaves were at least four times Desmond's height. The center fruiting stalk, however, was almost beyond belief. Although no thicker at the base than one of Desmond's thighs, the stalk extended at least a hundred feet above the ground. At the tip of the center stalk was a cluster of orange fruits.

For as far as Desmond could see, these plants dotted the savanna. The stalks of those in the distance resembled almost imperceptible vertical threads.

The three Outlanders stood beside the humans, gazing silently at the scene before them.

"This is amazing," Xavier said to the beings. "Thank you for bringing us to see it."

After the translation, Bard said. "We are pleased that you are pleased. However, you have not yet seen what we have come here to show you."

As the translation ended, all three Outlanders began pumping their arms, but this time more vigorously than usual. The resulting buzzes and clicks were so loud that Desmond had to cover his ears.

He noticed Lenny and Xavier were doing the same. The beings stopped as abruptly as they'd started.

Desmond lowered his hands. "What was that all about?"

Bard pumped his arms again, this time speaking at normal volume. "We have found the creatures to be curious. They hear us and they come nearer. You should now watch for them."

Desmond returned his gaze to the savanna. No sign of any animals.

Lenny said, "I guess you'd tell us if these creatures are dangerous, right?"

Bard replied, "They could be dangerous if you fail to get out of their way."

"Oh, great," Xavier muttered.

Desmond squinted. He'd been watching for things on the ground, but now he thought he saw movement above. There it was again. One of the tall stalks had actually moved. To its left another one was moving. The moving stalks, though, unlike the stationary ones, were missing their clumps of fruit. Instead, they had only a single small bulge at the very top.

"What in the name of Santa's shorts are those things?" Lenny exclaimed, almost in a whisper. Apparently, he was watching the moving stalks also, but Desmond wasn't willing to glance to the side to confirm this.

"I see them now!" Xavier said. "They're actually moving!"

The moving stalks began swaying back and forth, and soon Desmond spotted several more, all of them gently swaying left and right. Then he realized they were coming closer. Before long, the nearest was only a few hundred yards out, and as it came around from behind one of the tall plants that weren't moving, Desmond's eyes were drawn downward from its lofty tip just as its base came into view.

He let out a string of words without even being aware of what he was trying to say. The base of the hundred-foot-tall stalk was a creature's body. It was walking on four legs, each thicker than an elephant's leg.

Desmond then followed the stalk back upward. Although several feet thick at its base, the stalk gradually tapered until it was only a few inches in diameter. The bulge at its tip was actually the creature's head—a head not much bigger than Desmond's fist.

"Those lanky mofos are defying the laws of freaking physics," Lenny said. "No animal can hold a head up that high. It just ain't possible."

Yet there the creatures were, their heads held a hundred feet in the air. They kept coming, their necks gently swaying as they walked.

Bard spoke, and Desmond's translator said, "The plants grow their fruits high above the ground so the creatures cannot eat them. The creatures have grown their necks equally as high so they *can* eat them. We believe the plants will continue to grow higher, and therefore the creatures will grow taller. We do not know how many generations it has taken them to become this tall, but we will be interested to observe what happens to them in the future. We hope that you will be pleased to observe with us."

The creatures kept coming, at least eight that Desmond could see. Their elephant-sized bodies had the same general shape as the Outlanders' frog-steeds and the frog-beasts that had attacked Desmond's team on the hilltop: no tail, and sprawling hind legs that were longer than the forelegs. Other than their size and spectacularly long necks, they were generally frog-like.

The creatures came to a stop twenty yards from the group. They extended their necks outward and lowered their diminutive heads until Desmond was staring at eight tiny faces no more than an arm's length from his own face. Marble-sized eyes with lemon-yellow irises stared back at him. Their mouths were as wide as their faces, and each of them had bits of orange fruit skins stuck to their lips.

Bard spoke. "As I said, they are merely curious about us. You do not need to fear them."

One of the creatures opened its mouth and let out a soft, mewling cry, not unlike the sound a kitten would make when rubbing against someone's leg.

"Sweet baby Jesus!" Lenny muttered.

At that moment, Desmond realized something that had been eluding him since the arthropod world had been destroyed over a month ago. There was more to be found in the multiverse than violence, destruction, pain, and retribution.

19

———————

BRIDGERS

NINE AND A HALF years later - November 26

INFINITY STOOD with her arms crossed, watching the kids sparring with each other—human on human, Outlander on Outlander. She never allowed them to spar between species. Humans fighting with Outlanders was strictly forbidden at all times, even if it was just sparring in school.

"Sparkle, get your arms down lower," she instructed. "Beta has a clear shot at your gut. You wanna be punched in the gut?"

Sparkle made a face. "Beta's my friend, Miss Infinity. He won't punch my gut."

"He's your friend in real life, but this is pretend. You're pretending he's *not* your friend, remember? He's your enemy right now because he has come to this world seeking revenge on the Outlanders. You don't want him to hurt the Outlanders, do you?"

"But they're his friends too!"

Infinity sighed. Maybe five years old was too young to start school. "Beta, punch her in the gut."

Beta hesitated. Then he did it, although obviously pulling the punch. He was almost twice Sparkle's size.

Sparkle frowned. "Ow!"

Infinity resisted the urge to smile. "You see, kiddo? He's your enemy right now. Cover your gut, okay? But be ready to cover your face also if you need to."

Infinity gave a cursory glance at the three sparring pairs of Outlander kids. As usual, they were staying on task. She turned her attention then to the three other human pairs. Isla and Eden were doing okay, considering they were both six. Thorn and Phoenix, six and seven, seemed more interested in giggling than sparring. Infinity stepped closer to the pair showing the most hope for progress, Daisy and Alpha. Now ten years old, Daisy was learning fast. She was not only becoming a skilled fighter, she was also a patient teacher of the younger kids, and Alpha had been learning quickly from her.

Infinity watched the two go through their sets of jabs, kicks, and blocks. This activity was designed to build the kids' stamina without their hands or feet actually making contact. These two were getting old enough, though, to take decent hits without freaking out. "Daisy and Alpha, switch to contact sparring," she said.

Daisy's face was already flushed and glistening with sweat, but she smiled as if she'd been waiting all day for this. She narrowed her eyes at Alpha. "You want revenge on the Outlanders? You gotta go through me first, cupcake."

Lenny must have taught her that. Daisy, of course, had no idea what a cupcake was.

Alpha narrowed his eyes back at her. "*I'm* protecting the Outlanders, not you!" Alpha was only a year younger than Daisy, but he'd need more than a year's worth of maturing to catch up. He'd shown promise, but his temper sometimes got in his way.

Daisy did a decent feigned jab with her left hand and then

threw her right foot into Alpha's knee. "The Outlanders are under *my* protection, pipsqueak." She feigned again, this time with her right hand, and slapped the side of his head with her left.

Alpha lost it. He dove for her waist and took her to the floor. It was a good take-down, but then he simply held on, grunting and squeezing.

Daisy tried pushing him off. Then she punched the top of his head, which only made him squeeze harder. The other human and Outlander kids quit sparring and began gathering around, apparently realizing this was becoming a real fight.

Infinity let out a groan. She stepped over and pulled Alpha up by his shirt. The little shit still didn't let go.

Now Daisy was getting frustrated. She spread her arms wide and clapped Alpha's ears—hard.

He released her. "Damn you, Daisy! I'm telling my mom and dad!"

Infinity pulled him to his feet then got down on one knee, holding him by the shoulders. "Look at me, Alpha. Don't look at Daisy, look at me!"

He turned to her, huffing so hard he was snorting.

"You have to be able to spar without losing your temper, kiddo. This is all about self-discipline and self-control."

He glared at her. "You can't tell me what to do. You're not my mom. You're not *anybody's* mom!"

Several of the other kids inhaled loudly.

Infinity felt her face flush. Her hands tightened on his arms, and she had to force herself to relax.

Alpha seemed to realize what he'd just said. His eyes grew wide, and he tried unsuccessfully to pull away from her grip. "I didn't mean it, Miss Infinity." His lip was quivering.

"You listen to me carefully," she said.

He nodded.

"Me. Your mom. Your dad. Uncle Desmond. Grampy

Armando. All of us old people. We risked our lives to come here. Some actually died. We came from places where we had to fight and kill to survive. You need to be very, very glad that you never had to see or do those things. We're all here now, and this place is different. We do not hurt each other, and we do not hurt the Outlanders. Ever! You are learning to fight in case someone *else* comes here to hurt us or to hurt the Outlanders. Do you want someone to come here and kill you, or kill your mom and dad, and kill all your friends?"

He shook his head. "No."

"Well, someday they might. The only way we can stop them is to work together as one big family. Humans and Outlanders—together." She hesitated for a moment. "Are you afraid of me, Alpha?"

He nodded. "Yes."

"Don't be afraid of me. I'm your family. Daisy's your family. We all are. When people come here seeking revenge for what the old Outlanders did, who is going to keep them from killing you?"

"My family."

She drew him into her arms and hugged him fiercely. "That's right, kiddo. We all take care of each other."

"I'm sorry," he said, his voice strained by her tight embrace.

She released him and got to her feet. She scanned the faces of all the kids. "You guys, you're learning to fight for a reason. Your parents are learning to fight for a reason. If we're lucky, no one will come here for revenge, but if they do, we need to be ready. Right now, you're learning to fight with your hands. When you get older, you'll learn to fight with weapons. Someday there will be more of us, and we'll all be ready, just in case. There's one thing we *never* do! What is that?"

The answer came in practiced unison. "We don't hurt humans. We don't hurt Outlanders. We don't hurt our family!" Even the

Outlander kids participated in the chant, although with clicks and buzzes.

"Good. It's almost time for your history lesson, so finish your sparring exercises."

The oldest of the Outlander kids pumped his arms to speak. "I am as big as Daisy now. I fight Daisy today."

Infinity wasn't wearing a translator—all but two of those had been lost or broken years ago—but she understood the Outlander language well enough. The Outlanders also understood English, so the two species now conversed by speaking their own languages.

She shook her head. "No, Runner. The answer was no yesterday, it's no today, and it'll be no tomorrow. Humans never fight Outlanders. Not even when we're pretending. I'm pretty sure you know why."

Runner spoke again. "Okay, Miss Infinity. I fight Daisy the day after tomorrow."

Infinity sighed. Then a brief chuckle escaped her lips before she could stop it.

WHEN CELIA SHOWED up to take over with the kids' history lesson, Infinity decided not to tell her about Alpha's meltdown. Celia was well aware of her son's temper and didn't need the added stress of hearing about yet another incident. Besides, Infinity didn't feel like explaining what Alpha had said to her. Especially not on this particular day.

She left the school complex and made her way across the extensive walkway toward the residence complex. Armando had asked her to come by for lunch. She was pretty sure there was also another reason he'd invited her—for years he'd been doing the same thing on this very day.

Halfway across the walkway, she paused to gaze north. She

would never get tired of looking out over the sea. From this height she could see dozens of islands, scattered in no particular pattern, all the way to the horizon. No one could possibly explore them all, even in a hundred lifetimes. On the beach below, slightly to the west, stood the framework of the new Outlander city. After having observed construction of the human city on the hillside, the beings had quickly decided to use some of the new design ideas to construct an improved city of their own, this one only a half mile away. To Infinity, the new structure looked pretty much the same as the old one, but the Outlanders never missed an opportunity to express how thrilled they were with the modified design.

She was now standing almost directly above a twelve-inch pipe that ran from the underside of her city down to the swamp, where it dumped toilet waste into a 500-gallon capsule. This capsule was situated on rails that ran down to the beach. About four times per year, a lucky team selected by lottery had the privilege of pushing the capsule along the rails to the water's edge, tethering it to one of the humans' water vehicles, and towing it no less than twenty miles out to be emptied. This single sewage pipe and disposal method was perfectly fine for the current human population of twenty-nine, and probably would be for the rest of Infinity's life.

The city had come a long way, but Armando and Hayley always seemed to have plans for various improvements. Simple expansion was never a problem—just a matter of embedding a few more support pillars, snapping together pre-made framework pieces, and adding dwelling modules. However, Armando and Hayley had recently proposed rather ingenious plans for other improvements, such as an aerial tramway to get down to the beach and to the Outlander city without walking.

Before continuing along the walkway, Infinity paused and adjusted her shirt, which was made from thread-like fibers created in the Outlanders' factory. Even though Reyna was proficient at weaving the fibers into fabric and sewing functional garments,

Infinity had never quite gotten used to the scratchy fabric against her skin.

She made her way to the residence complex and rapped on Armando's door. The door swung open, and she was greeted by Hayley Millwright.

"Hi, Hayley. Um, I'm not interrupting anything, am I?"

Hayley flashed her famous smile. "No, no, no, of course not! We were expecting you."

Armando came up and put an arm around Hayley's waist. "Don't pretend like you didn't know we were an item, Infinity. Please, come in."

She entered the dwelling. How could she have missed this? It made perfect sense. Hayley's husband Alexander had died three years ago. Armando and Hayley were both over seventy, several decades older than any other humans on this planet. "I'm a freaking idiot." she said aloud.

"I don't think she knew, dear," Hayley said.

Armando was now walking to the back of the dwelling. "Preposterous! The girl knows me better than I know myself."

Hayley turned back to Infinity. "Armando tells me you're particularly fond of scallops, so we've prepared a real treat for you —seared, bacon-wrapped scallops."

Infinity inhaled the aroma. "Nice! But, um, bacon?"

"Well, let's call it *bacon of the sea.*" She held a hand to the side of her mouth like she was telling a secret. "We're experimenting with various parts of the sea sow." She was referring to a comical-looking aquatic salamander that spent its time walking along the sea floor grazing on algae and sea grass. The creature's flesh was generally thought to be unpalatable.

"Yummy!" Infinity said with mock enthusiasm.

Armando came up to her with something concealed behind his back. "Happy birthday, kiddo." He pulled the object from behind him and handed it over.

It was a spear. Not just any spear, but a carefully-crafted primitive weapon. It had a stone spearpoint that Armando had apparently flintknapped by hand. The spearhead had been expertly notched then wrapped securely to the wooden shaft with a strip of what appeared to be monkey-frog leather.

"This is amazing, Armando! Thank you. It's also a telltale sign of a man who has too much time on his hands."

"Preposterous," he said again. "I only wish there were more hours in each day."

For past birthdays, Armando had made Infinity three stone knives, two stone axes, and a vicious-looking chopping weapon fashioned from the toothed jawbone of a crocodile-salamander. Infinity loved them all. She and Desmond had found a special spot on one of the walls of their dwelling to display each weapon, with the hope that there would never be a need to use them.

Armando put his hands on Infinity's upper arms. "Here's the God-sworn truth, kiddo. Your birthdays are more special to me than my own, and this one—this one is meaningful in ways you may not imagine. You are now forty."

She bit her lip. "Is this supposed to cheer me up? Because I don't really need—"

He cut her off by shaking her slightly by the arms. "Embrace who you are! You're the bedrock of this colony. You turning forty is symbolic to all of us. We've endured and triumphed on this world for nearly a decade." He released her and waved at the walls and ceiling. "Just look what we've accomplished. It's all quite staggering, to be honest."

She forced a half-smile and nodded once. "Yes it is, but your praise for me isn't—"

"I know what you're thinking," he said, cutting her off again. He tapped a finger to her forehead. "I know what goes on in there. You're acutely aware that you are now forty and still haven't had children. When it comes to me, you're also aware that you haven't provided me with grandchildren. It was idiotic of me to have ever told you that's what I wanted from you. Idiotic. We're surrounded by fourteen beautiful children here, with more on the way. We're practically up to our necks in rugrats. More than enough for all of us to enjoy."

"Armando, I'm well beyond caring that Desmond and I haven't had our own kids. Perhaps someday Kitty will come here, and then I can ask her why the procedure didn't work. Most likely, though, her people won't ever show up, at least not during our lifetimes. The fact of the matter is, I've always known I'm not suited to being a mother. The events nine years ago convinced me of that. I'm genetically predisposed to revenge—and probably violence in general. Hell, I almost destroyed any chance for our colony to live on this world."

He pursed his lips and sighed through his nose. He tapped her forehead again. "Yet, I know what goes on in there." He paused for a moment and glanced at Hayley before turning back to Infinity. "I have something to tell you. My purpose for doing so is to help you understand why I have no reason to be disappointed that you haven't given me grandchildren. Do you want to know a secret?"

"Do I have a choice?"

He smiled and wagged a finger at her. "Very intuitive. This is a particularly juicy morsel of truth, and so help me God you're going to keep it to yourself. Kapish?"

She rolled her eyes and nodded.

"Sparkle, Phoenix, and the two little ones, Pearl and Coral."

Infinity nodded. "Yeah, Donica and Latonya's kids." Armando had named the four children the two wildcards had birthed and were now raising. The other two wildcards, Sue and Tessa, became Gideon's mates long ago, but Donica and Latonya eventually moved into a dwelling together and were still happy living that way.

"It is generally believed among the others," Armando said, "that Richard is the biological father."

Infinity nodded again.

"That is an incorrect belief," Armando said.

Infinity felt her eyes growing wide. "What? Are you serious?"

"Don't act so shocked. I happen to have highly-desirable genetic material. Donica and Latonya told me I was their first choice."

Hayley stepped up beside Armando and slipped an arm around his shoulders. "He's actually highly desirable in many different ways."

Infinity thrust out a hand, palm out. "Okay, enough! It's bad enough you're feeding me sea sow bacon."

—

THE HIGHEST POINT of the human city was a viewing platform some ten feet above the residence complex. Infinity and Desmond climbed to the platform most evenings to watch the sunset. On this particular evening, of course, it was a must. In fact, they'd arrived early and had been sitting in silence for the last half hour, gazing out at the islands and watching the Outlanders swim around among the corals.

At any given moment, there were always a few Outlanders in the water, swimming simply for pleasure or for collecting and monitoring their underwater livestock. Their livestock were actually hundreds of sea cucumbers, creatures Desmond fondly referred to as *donkey dung cucumbers* because each individual looked like a foot-long piece of poop. That's also what they tasted like, at least to Infinity—the Outlanders considered them delicious.

Infinity turned to the west just as the sun started to touch the horizon. She thought of ancient seafaring humans on her own home version of Earth. Had they believed the sun actually sank beneath the sea each night? Perhaps they had imagined it was extinguished by the water, only to be reignited each morning by some kind of torch-wielding god.

"Happy fortieth, my love," Desmond said, breaking the silence.

She turned to him. He now wore his hair long, pulled back into a ponytail, just as he had before his first bridging excursion a decade ago. Although he was now only thirty-nine, his hair was streaked with numerous gray strands. "I feel like I've lived a lot longer," she said.

"Yeah. The things we've seen...."

She contemplated this for a moment. "I was thinking about that today. I love where we are and who we are at this moment, but all the shit we had to go through to get to this point? I just hope our kids never have to experience anything like it."

His eyes met hers. "Our kids?"

"You know what I mean. All our kids. I had to remind Alpha this morning that we're one big family, and we don't ever hurt each other."

Desmond huffed a brief laugh. "What'd Alpha do this time?"

"Nothing he hasn't done before. It's his temper."

He turned back toward the sea. A few seconds later he pointed. "Look out there at it all, Passerina."

She gazed out over the patchwork of islands and water, which was now bathed in the sunset's orange glow.

He went on. "I think our kids—at least the adventurous ones— won't be all that different from you and me. Every one of those islands is unique, with its own terrain and endemic lifeforms. As far as I can tell, they go on forever. Infinite new worlds to explore. In their own way, our kids are going to be bridgers."

Infinity blinked and shook her head slightly as she stared out at the sea. She'd never really thought of that. Desmond had once again shown that he viewed the world through his own unique lens. When she looked at the islands, she could only assess the possible dangers. Almost involuntarily, her mind would sort through various strategies for finding shelter and fashioning weapons, choosing the most feasible combination to allow survival until she could get herself and those with her the hell out of there and back to a safer place. Desmond, however, saw only adventure and wondrous possibilities.

With just a few well-chosen words, he had given her a gift, a new way to look at her purpose on this world.

Everyone in the colony had eventually found new purpose for their lives—their own paths to absolution—and Infinity had found hers. Her job, and her passion, was to teach the colony's kids the importance of peace, something they could pass down to their own kids, ensuring that history didn't repeat itself. Also, her responsibility was to prepare the kids for whatever dangers they might face. She was teaching them to fight when fighting was the only choice.

Now, Desmond had astutely pointed out an aspect of her job she hadn't even considered—she was preparing future bridgers.

Infinity's lips moved as she silently recalled words she hadn't spoken in many years. The words came to her easily. The Bridger's Creed, after all, was embedded within every cell of her body and would be until her last day.

She chewed her lip, considering the creed. Yes, it could be done. She only needed to change a few words. She would teach the creed to the colony's children—a creed for a new generation of bridgers.

Heart to blood, muscle to bone, family flesh above my own.
With self-sacrifice near, my fuel is fear.
By bridger means and might, my family will not fight.
I aspire to inspire before I expire.
Bide within the law I must, in untainted family trust.

Yes, ***Bridgers 6: The Bond of Absolution*** is the last book in the Bridgers series, but have you read all the others? Don't miss ***Bridgers 1-5***. Also, don't miss the series prequel, ***INFINITY: A Bridger's Origin***, the story of how Infinity became a bridger!

And you're also going to want to check out my ***Diffusion series***, my ***Across Horizons series***, and my ***Fused series***.

INFINITY: A Bridger's Origin

Infinite worlds. Extreme danger. One fearless woman.

Passerina Fowler just wants to be a professional fighter. She has struggled for years to make a name for herself. But then her life abruptly changes when she's discovered by a recruiter from Safe-Trek Bridging, a company that transports clients to alternate versions of Earth.

With nothing to lose, Passerina accepts a job as a bridger, an elite fighter who protects clients on excursions to alternate worlds. However, on her first day she witnesses a horrifying event and realizes bridging can be downright deadly.

In spite of the risks, she is determined to complete her training program. But she soon realizes the training is more focused on her fears than her strength and endurance. And for good reason—there is much to be feared when bridging to alternate worlds naked and unarmed. Passerina must steadily transform herself into a bridger, with a new name: Infinity.

Infinity grows impatient for the excitement and danger of her first bridging excursion. But when it finally comes, she finds herself in a world of vicious predators, and the danger becomes all too real.

AUTHOR'S NOTES

Some of you may have questions. So, I decided to offer my thoughts on a few things related to **Bridgers 6: The Bond of Absolution**. These topics are in no particular order, and they may not even be important to most people. But if you are at all interested, here you go.

Is it really possible a version of Earth could develop with Amphibians but without reptiles, birds, or mammals? Not only is this possible, it is probable. If Earth had a do-over of the last 360 million years (which is the divergence point of the version of Earth featured in Bridgers 6), the planet would most likely have amphibians today, because amphibians already existed 360 million years ago. However, reptiles, birds, and mammals did not exist 360 million years ago. So, there would be *very* little chance that these groups would evolve on that world *again*. Why? Because evolutionary events are based upon mutations (changes in the DNA passed on to offspring), and mutations are random. When a sexually reproducing animal or plant produces offspring, those offspring are all different from each other. Some of these differences are due to random mutations. Most mutations have little or no effect, but a few result in some kind of difference in the creature's body. Most of these differences are bad for the offspring, but occasionally one of them results in a change that actually helps the offspring survive. Those offspring then have a better chance of producing their own offspring, and eventually, creatures that have this new feature replace those that don't have the feature. This is how gradual changes occur over many generations.

But my point is, these gradual changes (and even occasional fast changes) are *random*. So, it's highly unlikely that reptiles (for example) would emerge again. Consider this: Amphibians emerged about 375 million years ago. Reptiles emerged 55 to 65 million years after that (at about 320 to 310 million years ago). In a do-over of Earth that begins 360 million years ago, amphibians would already exist, so they're probably going to stick around until today. However, this other Earth is on a *different* timeline from ours for all those 360 million years! On our version of Earth, it took 65 million years after amphibians emerged for reptiles to emerge. During these 65 million years on our hypothetical alternate Earth, random mutations are *not* going to produce reptiles *again*. That would be almost impossible, right? It would be even more impossible for mammals (210 million years ago) or birds (60 million years ago) to emerge.

So, we wouldn't expect to see reptiles, mammals, or birds on that alternate world, but we would probably see *other* types of creatures that have emerged in the last 360 million years. These creatures would be every bit as fantastic as reptiles, birds, and mammals, but they wouldn't actually *be* reptiles, birds, and mammals. They would be something else. On the world of Bridgers 6, many of them look similar to amphibians, but they probably wouldn't actually *be* amphibians. Instead, they would be some of these amazing categories of animals that gradually emerged due to random mutations over the past 360 million years. We have such things as monkey-frogs, whale-salamanders, frog-steeds, and an incredible elephant-sized creature that can hold its head up a hundred feet in the air.

Whew! Fascinating stuff, but it makes my head spin.

Is it really possible that an animal could have a neck that long? The creatures at the end of Bridgers 6 can hold their heads 100 feet high. At first glance, this may seem impossible. After all, the longest neck on Earth today is the giraffe's, and the tallest giraffe is only about 20 feet tall (and the giraffe's neck is only 8 feet long). But did you know there were sauropods (those really big dinosaurs) with necks that were 50 feet long? That's six times longer than the longest giraffe neck. And considering the height of the sauropod's body, that adds another 11.5 feet... so the tallest sauropod could reach up to about 62 feet in the air!

Sauropods had a number of adaptations that made this possible. First, they had a lot of neck bones (vertebrae), up to 19 (almost all mammals, including giraffes, have no more than seven). Also, the sauropod neck bones were hollow, making their necks lighter and easier to hold up.

One of the problems with having a really long neck is breathing. It is very difficult to breath through a long, long tube. Just try breathing through a 50-foot garden hose—your lungs cannot push the air all the way through the hose, so you end up inhaling the same air you exhaled. Well, scientists believe that sauropods could breath like birds, in which they could draw fresh air into their lungs continuously, instead of having to breathe out before breathing in (like mammals have to do).

So, imagine a creature with a body as large as an elephant's, with a thick, muscular neck at the base but tapering upward all the way to a tiny, fist-sized head. The bones of the neck are hollow, and the upper neck and head are very small, making it extremely light. The creatures breathes like a bird. And therefore, they can eat the fruits of a plant 100 feet high (20 feet of body, 80 feet of neck). Pardon the pun, but that's not too much of a stretch, is it?

Is it really possible to chemically cook meat using the juice of a fruit? Absolutely. Trish and I like to make *ceviche*, a food that we became familiar with in Belize and Costa Rica. Ceviche is made with raw seafood (often fish, shrimp, or conch meat). Lime juice is added to chemically "cook" the meat. This happens because lime juice is very acidic. The acid in the lime juice chemically denatures the proteins in your fish, similar to the way the proteins are denatured when heated. If you haven't tried ceviche, I recommend it!

What about this crazy idea that there is a Revenge Gene? This is a much more complex question than you might think. First of all, some scientists suggest that there is an evolutionary element to the desire for revenge (in other words, we have developed a tendency for revenge because that tendency is in some way helpful to our chances of surviving to produce offspring). For example, it has been shown that people are more likely to carry out revenge when other people are watching. Presumably, this is because we think that if people see that we can be hurt without hurting back, they will assume we are weak, and therefore other people will not be afraid to hurt us. If there is actually an evolutionary tendency for revenge, then revenge is in our DNA (it's genetic). If it's in our DNA, then there has to be variation in how much it is expressed from one person to the next (variation between individuals is what DNA is all about). So, by this logic, there is indeed a "revenge gene" (although there is probably more than one single gene that is involved). Some people are predisposed to revenge, others much less so.

Other studies suggest that people who are naturally more aggressive (they tend to hurt people because they enjoy hurting people) are more likely to seek revenge. In this case, if there is a genetic component to being naturally aggressive, then there are "genes" for revenge. Infinity is a much more aggressive person than Desmond, therefore she has more of a tendency toward revenge. But her case is an easy one to explain. What about Celia, and Lenny, Richard, Xavier, and the others who were overwhelmed by the desire for revenge against the Outlanders? Lenny's not a naturally aggressive person, is he? Perhaps this can be explained by the fact that many people do not exist in circumstances in which they have easy opportunities to express their naturally-aggressive nature. Infinity grew up fighting. Lenny has never been in a fight in his life (until the first time he bridged to an alternate world.

On the other side of the coin, some studies show that *forgiveness* is an evolutionary trait. If so, then it has a genetic basis and you would expect to find variation in this tendency between individuals. So, not only is there a "revenge gene," there is also a "forgiveness gene."

The Outlanders communicate by moving their arms, creating clicks and buzzes. Is it possible to communicate this way? This is exactly how many insects communicate. In fact, the Outlanders' *tymbals* are modeled after the tymbals of cicadas. A tymbal is a stiff, corrugated structure on the cicada's exoskeleton. The cicada can contract certain muscles, which buckles the tymbal, creating the clicks and buzzes we are familiar with. This is a highly-evolved form of communication (although certainly not a language of a sentient being). Even in places where multiple species of cicadas are calling, the female cicadas can tell which of the calls are from males of their own species. Humans use their mouths to speak, but there is no reason why other sentient species wouldn't be able to use vastly different ways of creating language sounds.

Why did Colonel Chislett tell two of the wildcards to hide guns in the supply boxes, when Kitty had specifically told the humans not to take weapons? Colonel Chislett did not fully understand the capabilities of Kitty's people. He assumed they would not detect the firearms. We don't know for sure, but it is likely that he simply wanted the human migrants to have the best possible chance of surviving. In his mind, that could only be done by arming the migrants.

Did Kitty actually bridge the migrants to the world she promised she'd bridge them to? Although Infinity doubted this at first, it eventually became evident that the humans were sent to the originally-promised world. Kitty said there would be another sentient species on this world, and indeed there is. What she *didn't* tell them was that this sentient species consisted of genetic copies (clones) of Outlanders, the species that destroyed Earth. That's a really important detail to leave out, don't you think?

Why didn't Infinity become pregnant? There are plenty of possible reasons. First, it's possible that Kitty didn't actually fix the damage to Infinity's reproductive system (either on purpose or by accident). Second, it's possible that Desmond's sperm cell count is extremely low, or that he may have some other reproductive deficiency. And third, it could just be bad luck. Or good luck, depending on how you look at it. Infinity has become convinced that she doesn't deserve to have her own children. Maybe she is relieved that she hasn't become pregnant. Or maybe—just maybe—Kitty did something else to her body instead of fixing her damage. Hmm...

Did Gibson (and perhaps the other wildcards) intend to persuade the other migrants to adopt their lifestyle? With Gibson gone, we may never know. But Desmond and the others, in retrospect, have come to believe Gibson wasn't as bad as they had originally thought. This is an example of people letting their preconceptions cloud their judgement. We're all human, including Infinity and Desmond, and it happens. The wildcards were new to their "family" and were added to the list of migrants at the last minute under mysterious circumstances (no explanation given). On top of that, Gibson had a somewhat confrontational personality, and then he admitted to having murdered at least one other man in order to win his four mates (shocking, to say the least). As a result, the other migrants (especially Infinity) assumed the wildcards were going to be nothing but trouble.

Are the Outlanders exact genetic copies of their ancestors who developed bridging technology and destroyed entire civilizations? Yes. The original Outlanders lived tens of thousands of years ago, in a different part of the galaxy. Not only did they decide it was up to them to determine which civilizations should be allowed to live (in other words, they thought of themselves as gods), they were also vain enough to try to achieve a form of immortality by embedding their genetic codes into the instructions they broadcast by radio signal. Apparently, Kitty's people admire the Outlanders to the point of almost worshipping them. Kitty's people were thrilled to discover the Outlanders' hidden genetic codes in the signal. So thrilled, in fact, that they actually studied the codes until they could create clones of the Outlanders. They established colonies of these clones on several alternate versions of Earth, hoping at least one of the colonies would thrive and eventually become an awe-inspiring civilization similar to that of their original ancestors. Then, however, Kitty's people discovered that the original Outlanders could only thrive in the presence of another sentient species, in a sort of mutualistic relationship. The other species, it seems, served the purpose of focusing the Outlanders' thoughts, which tended to stray in seemingly random directions. So, Kitty's people decided they needed to introduce another sentient species to each of the Outlander clone colonies. For this world, they chose Desmond, Infinity, and the other migrants.

Will these Outlanders eventually become like their genetic ancestors? If they do, this could be a huge problem. But Infinity, Desmond, and the other migrants are determined to make sure this never happens. They are teaching the colony's children, as well as the Outlander children, about the dangers of becoming like the original Outlanders. And they hope this attitude is passed on generation after generation, forever preventing either species from becoming tempted to carry out such heinous crimes.

Is Bridgers 6 really the last in the series? Yes, that's my plan at this time. From the beginning, this was planned as a six-book series. After numerous readers requested Infinity have her own book, I decided to add **INFINITY: A Bridger's Origin** to the series, making a total of seven books. Could I be convinced to write more? Absolutely. But for now, I'm planning a new series, with the first book coming out in early 2020. Don't worry, the new series will involve amazing creatures, mysterious wilderness areas, and plenty of action. And there will even be just the right amount of romance. After all, love is the tie that binds us, right? No matter how different we are. Even if we aren't of the same species (oops, I think I let a hint slip out).

ACKNOWLEDGMENTS

I am not capable of creating a book such as this on my own. I have the following people, among others, to thank for their assistance.

First I wish to thank Monique Agueros for her help with editing. She has a keen eye for typos, poorly structured sentences, misplaced commas, and errors of logic. If you find a sentence or detail in the book that doesn't seem right, it is likely because I failed to implement one of her suggestions.

My wife Trish is always the first to read my work, and therefore she has the burden of seeing my stories in their roughest form. Thankfully, she kindly points out where things are a mess. Her suggestions are what get the editing process started. She also helps with various promotional efforts. And finally, she not only tolerates my obsession with writing, she actually encourages it.

I also owe thanks to those on my Advance Reviewer team. They were able to point out numerous typos and inconsistencies, and they are all-around fabulous people!

Finally, I am thankful to all the independent freelance designers out there who provide quality work for independent authors such as myself. Jake Caleb Clark (www.jcalebdesign.com) created the awesome cover for *Bridgers 6: The Bond of Absolution*.

ABOUT THE AUTHOR

Stan Smith has lived most of his life in the Midwest United States and currently resides with his wife Trish in a house deep in an Ozark forest in Missouri. He writes adventure novels that have a generous sprinkling of science fiction. His novels and stories are about regular people who find themselves caught up in highly unusual situations. They are designed to stimulate your sense of wonder, get your heart pounding, and keep you reading late into the night, with minimal risk of exposure to spelling and punctuation errors. His books are for anyone who loves adventure, discovery, and mind-bending surprises.

Stan's Author Website
http://www.stancsmith.com

Feel free to email Stan at: stan@stancsmith.com
He loves hearing from readers and will answer every email.